BEYOND THE BOUNDARY FENCE

STEFAN TAYLOR

Melbourne, Australia

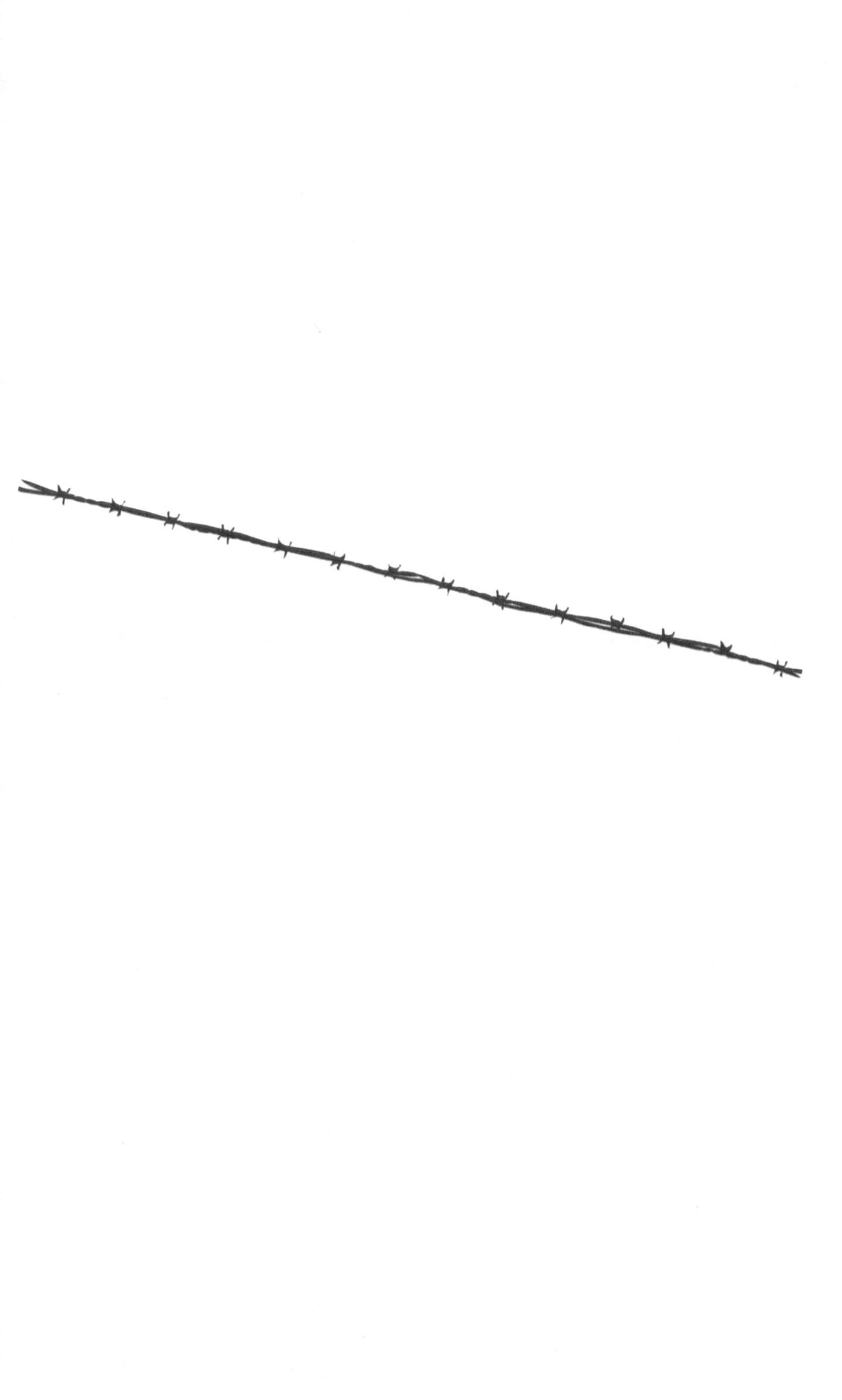

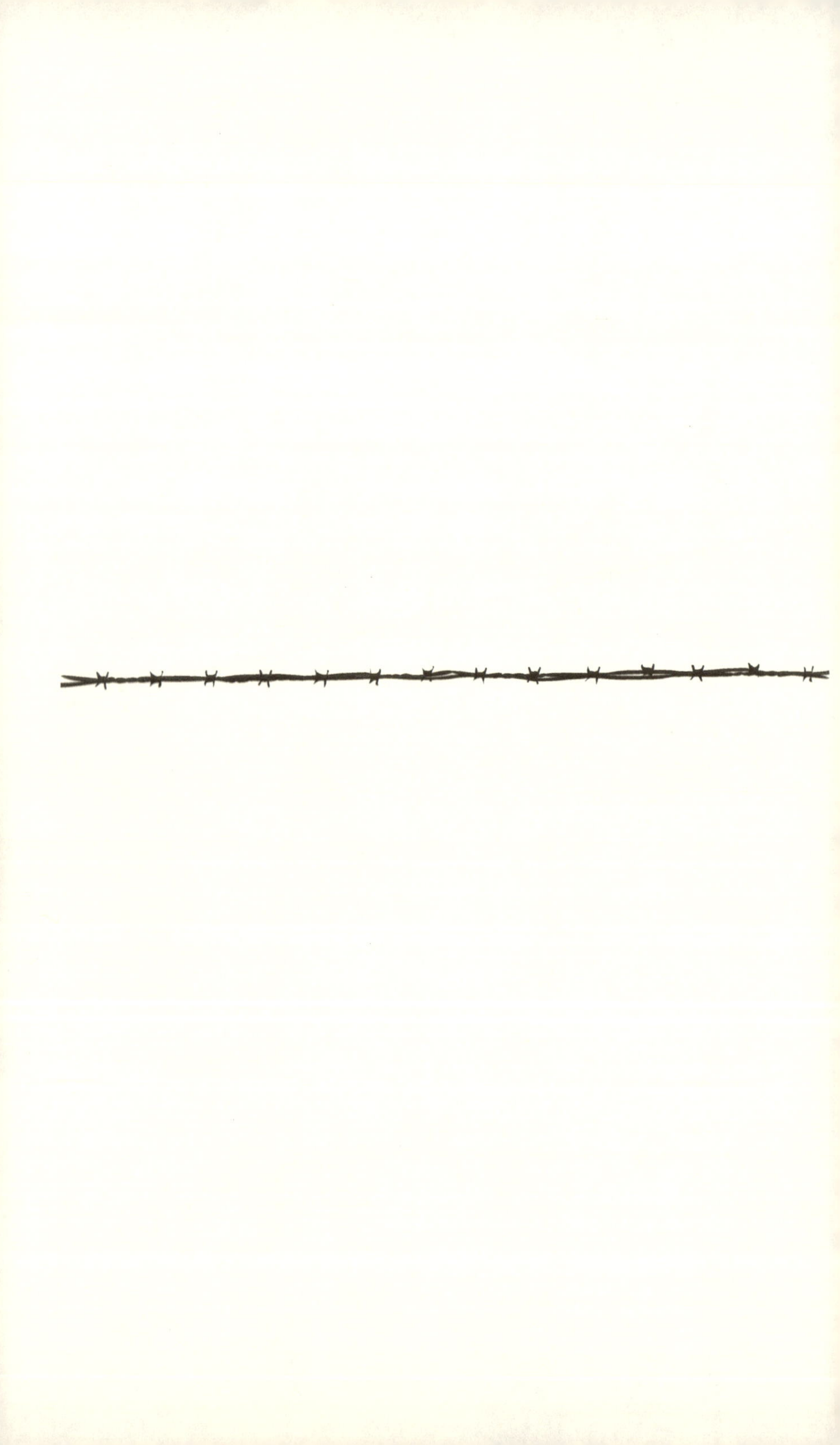

Dedicated to
Herbert 'Peter' Taylor.
We still miss you, 'Old Pete.'

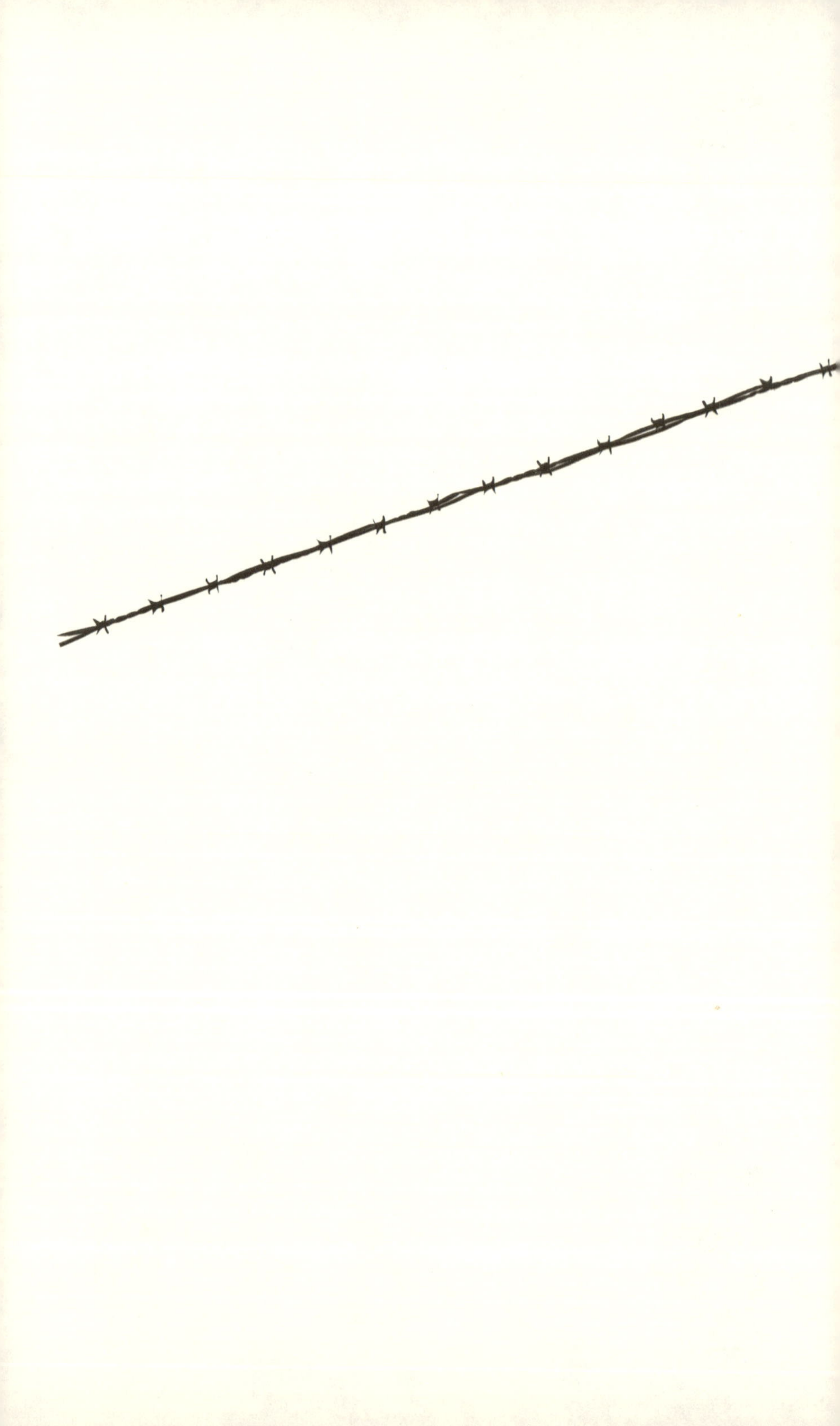

CHAPTER 1

The sun was bright and the breeze was cool, the perfect conditions for a hike. Martin had been a hiker all his life, and loved finding new areas to explore. He wished the kids had come along, but they were older now and busy with Twitter and Facebook, or whatever it was kids were doing these days. His wife had told him he should take it easy on his hikes; he was about to turn fifty after all. But when you worked forty-plus hours a week in a stuffy office with stuffy people, the chance to get away from the big city was a Godsend.

In his hurry to get a good day's hike in, he had not actually told anyone where he was heading. Martin knew this was not the smartest thing to do, but still he was only ever a few kilometres from any residential areas. Although there was no trail as such, he was a very confident map-reader; he had even won the orienteering competition in his scout days.

Martin took the compass from his pocket and got his bearings. The new housing estate, what was it called again?

Golden Plains or Pastures, should be just over the far ridge. He shoved the compass back in his pocket and powered on.

The sun had disappeared over the ridge when Martin came to a stop in a shadowy clearing. In the centre was a house, it may have been a grand dwelling once but now it was little more then a rusty mess. Bits of the roof had come away and the roots of the surrounding trees had pushed their way through the veranda. The paintwork had pealed, giving the place the look of an animal shedding its skin. The building was three-storeys high with a small spire that reached just above the tree line. The windows were dark and coated with dust, making it impossible to see what might be inside. Everywhere else the setting sun bathed the bushland in deep, rich colours. Except here. Martin was not a man to be unnerved but there was something about this old place that seemed wrong, and he suddenly felt the urge to get as far away as possible.

Yes, there was definitely something wrong. That house shouldn't be there.

A sound interrupted his thoughts. He listened. It came again, soft like a whisper.

There it was again. It seemed to be coming from somewhere in the bush. But Martin couldn't pinpoint the source. *It must be the breeze through the trees.*

He went to take a step, but his legs refused to obey. He tried to move again, but couldn't. It was as if his muscles had frozen. With a huge effort, he managed to turn his head and look back to the clearing.

The…thing…that stood opposite him, partly obscured by

the thick bushes, turned Martin's blood to ice in a heart beat. His stomach tightened and he felt a warm trickle down his leg.

He willed himself to run but he couldn't move! He wanted to yell for help, but all he could manage was a stifled gasp. Again, that sound. A whisper so close it felt like it was inside his head – terrible and soothing all at once… He shook his head; it was speaking to him, that thing was speaking to him!

Slowly, it emerged from the bushes. Every part of Martin's body was screaming at him to run. But it was impossible to resist the whisper. Step by slow step Martin found himself walking towards it. He couldn't have resisted even if he wanted to, the whispers continued to call him forward until he stood just meters from the hulking creature.

It reached out and wrapped an icy hand about his throat, pulling his head close to its own. The whispers became horribly clear, screaming in his mind.

Join us, join us, join us, it said, over and over again.

The thing dragged Martin toward the bush line. But then it stopped, and spun to face the old house. It hissed at one of the high windows before continuing on.

From within the old house, Martin caught a glimpse of a figure turning away from the window. He tried to yell for help, but it was no use. He was now completely paralysed, a prisoner in his own body. The creature dragged him into the bush.

Martin caught a last look at the sun, and then everything went dark as he felt himself slip into unconsciousness.

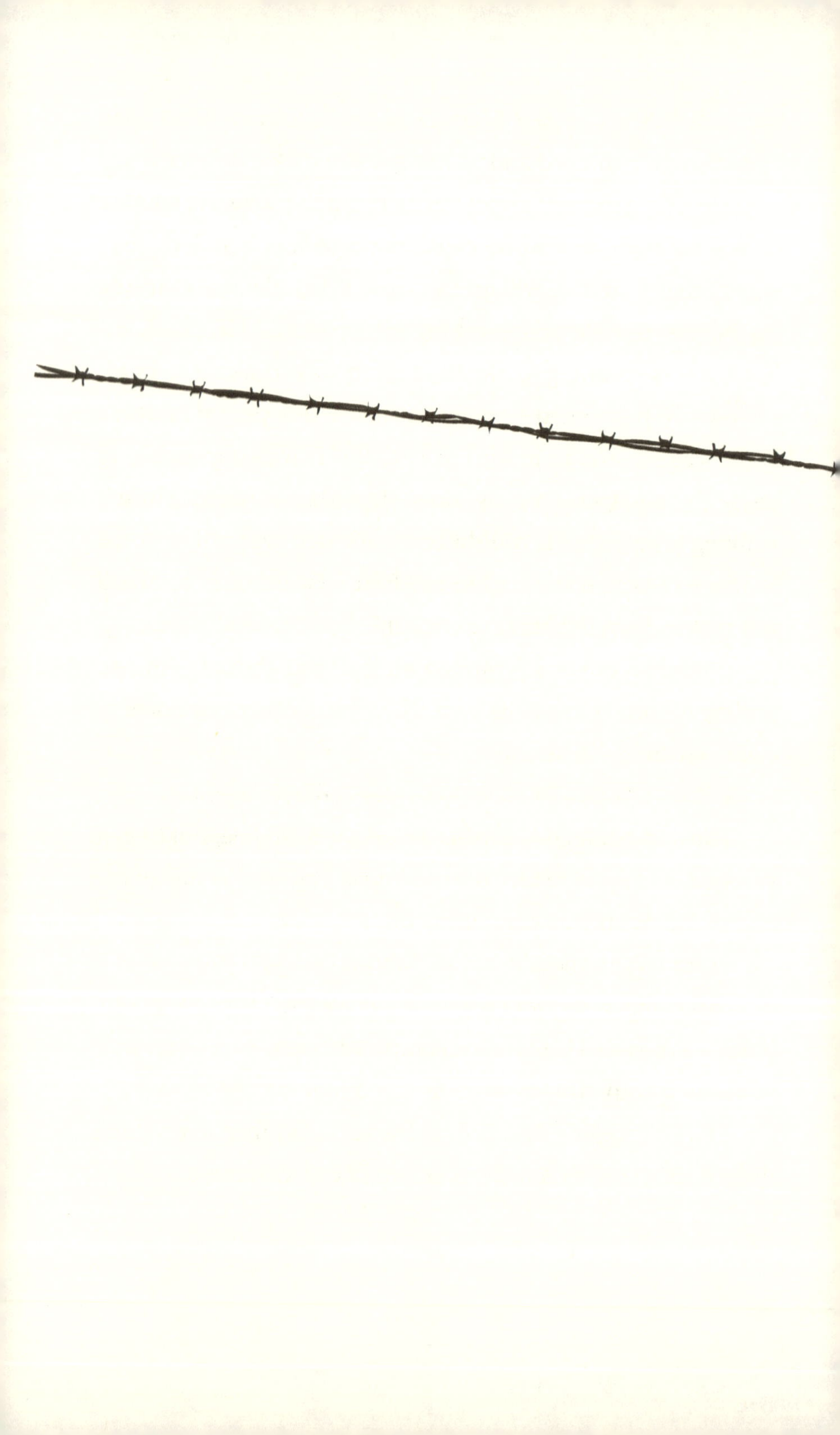

CHAPTER 2

The suburb named Golden Pastures was exactly like all the other new, developments on the far outskirts of the city; absolutely nothing like its name suggested. It was too far from the city to be a proper suburb, and not quite deep enough in the bush to be a country town. Still, it was new, clean…ish, and cheap. Or, as the company who built it liked to say: 'Humble'.

Row upon row of large white and earth-brown houses lined the streets like silent sentries. And despite the fact that the area was growing fast, the streets always seemed empty, except for the late afternoon winds that blew in from the mountains.

At the back of one of the houses sat Brody Webb. He was short and skinny for a 14 year old, making him an easy target for the other kids at the various schools he'd attended in his short life. He couldn't remember a year he hadn't been the target of bullies. He'd almost gotten used to it…almost. But this year would be different. He had a new house, a new school, a new beginning. And for a short while, his new home at Golden

Pastures had been the exciting new start it promised. Brody's dad had been working more and drinking less, and his mother had lost the worn-down look she carried.

For a while, things had been good.

But then the trucking company his dad worked for had made cuts, leaving his old man unemployed. Again. It hadn't taken long for him to crawl back into the bottom of a beer bottle.

As a result his mum took on the more highly-paid position of night shift at the factory, which brought in a whopping, two dollars seventy more an hour. The worn-down look had etched its self back on her face, and things had slowly returned to the way they had always been.

Now Brody sat at the back of the small house listening to his parents argue, a song he heard most afternoons before his mum left for work. A heavy weight had sat it's self in his stomach, anchoring him to the spot. He felt like crying, but he had to be strong – not that he really knew what that meant. But he was pretty sure *not* crying was a good start.

His parents arguing had swelled to its crescendo; the front door slammed as his mother left for work, and silence descended.

The heavy footfalls marked the approach of Brody's dad. He tensed as the screen door swung open and the six-foot giant stared down at him.

"That's where you been hiding, huh?" he took a swig from the beer bottle he held, swaying slightly as he did. Brody stood and tried to push past the giant but a large hand stopped him in his tracks. "I don't think so. There's no way you're sitting inside watching the box all night, go find something to do."

Brody tried to pass again; this time the giant shoved him back. "I'm serious, I don't want you here I'm sick of you stuffing around the house. I told your mum, we should find you some work over the holidays."

Father and son eyed each other for a long moment before the giant's voice cut the silence. "Ah, go on piss off! Find something to do, lazy little prick."

Brody tried once more to push past the giant, but the big man shoved him back hard. "You deaf as well as dumb? I said, piss off!"

This time Brody broke into a run, sprinting down the side of the house; he grabbed his rusted old bike from its spot by the fence, and rode as hard as his thin legs would let him. As he disappeared into the maze of streets, he still wouldn't let the tears flow.

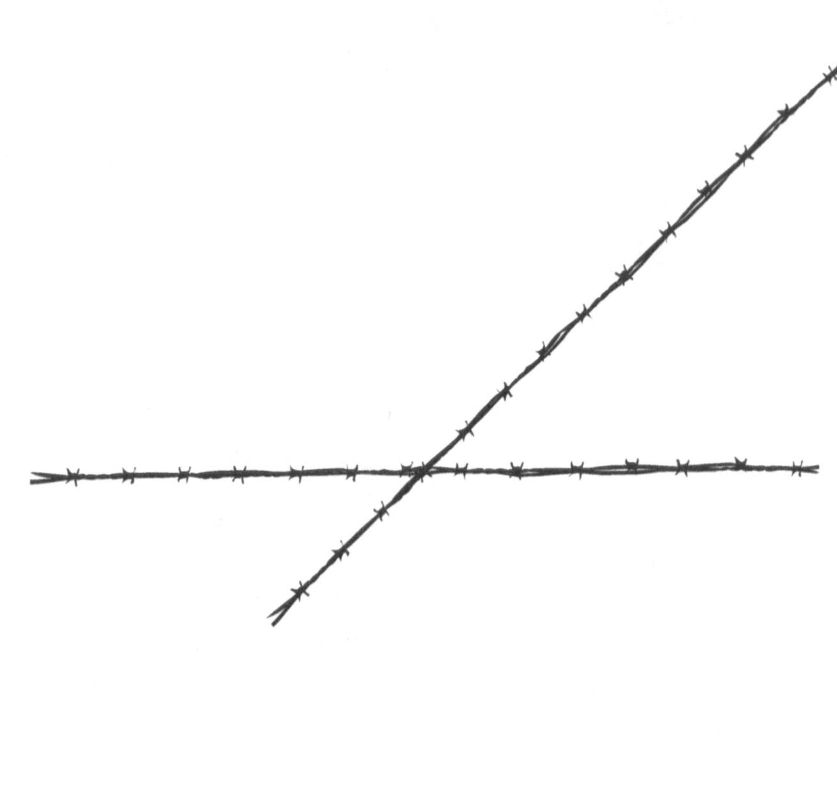

CHAPTER 2

rody sped along the wide streets of the estate ignoring the burning in his legs. His only thought was to get as far away from the giant as possible. He didn't notice the tall kid peddle into his path until it was too late.

They collided with a resounding 'clang,' as the two bikes bounced off each other. The next thing Brody knew, he was flat on his back looking at the sky, his head spinning.

"Are you okay, Todd?" said a distant voice.

"Yeah, I just sliced my knee," said another.

"What about that kid?"

"I'm going to smash him. Look at my bike, it's a wreck!"

"It's hardly got a scratch on it," said a girl's voice.

Brody heard footsteps approaching. He tried to sit up but his head was still spinning.

"Yeah, smash him Todd!" said the first voice.

A strong hand grabbed Brody's shirt and he found himself face-to-face with a boy about his own age but bigger, a lot bigger. A shorter boy and a girl flanked him.

"What do you think you're doing?" said the tall boy, "You almost ran into Zoe!"

Brody tried to stammer a response, but knew that nothing was going to save him from the beating that was coming.

"Todd, stop! It was an accident," pleaded the girl.

"Hit him Todd, do it!" the other boy said excitedly.

Brody tried to speak again but no words came. Suddenly the big boy's grip loosened as the girl stepped between them.

"That's enough," she said. "What the hell is wrong with you? It was an accident, he didn't see us," she pushed Todd away before rounding on the other boy, "And you, stop egging him on!"

The other boy looked like he'd just got a dressing down from his mother. The girl took a tissue from her pocket and stuffed it into Brody's hand. "Here, your nose is bleeding." She looked him over, "You got a name or what?" she asked.

"Brody."

"Right, well, I'm Zoe, this is Todd and the weirdo over there is Mike. You local?"

"Yeah, I live a few blocks over from the Bush line," he said, still tense and waiting for the first punch to land.

"So what's your big hurry? You could've killed us, dickhead," said Todd.

"I'm sorry. I just had to get away from..."

"From what?" Zoe asked.

"Nothing, I'm sorry if I messed your bike up, I...I better go."

Watched by the others, Brody untangled his bike and tried to peddle away, but the chain had broken and the wheels wouldn't turn. The others laughed and Brody felt his face flush with embarrassment.

"Looks like you're walking," laughed Zoe as she made her way over. "Here, let me see." Brody was unsure what she meant for a moment, but before he could say anything, she had flipped the bike and was examining the busted chain with the eyes of an expert. Mike and Todd joined her.

"What do ya reckon Zo, fixable?" asked Todd.

"Yeah easy, I can fix this at my place. You guys want to come over? My parents won't be home till late."

"Sounds good!" Mike said.

He and Zoe turned and began walking down the street, Zoe wheeling Brody's bike. Todd picked up his own bike and hopped on before turning to Brody, "Well, come on, what are you waiting for?"

Brody hesitated, he was still a little dizzy from his fall and he wasn't sure what was going on. Were these kids really inviting him to hang out? No, it was a trap; they were going to bash him!

"I think I should head home actually…"

"Don't be stupid, we're going to fix that shit-box of yours."

But Brody wasn't convinced; he eyed the taller boy warily. "You're not going to bash me?"

"Why would I do that?"

"Because I crashed into you."

"That was before. Come on, we're going to fix your bike," he said.

"Why are you helping me?" Brody asked.

"You're a local like us, right? Well, we look out for locals.

Plus this place is boring as, unless you've got people to hang out with."

"What's the hold up?" Zoe called.

"Keep your undies on!" Todd yelled back, "Come hang out, man; Zoe's place is only down the street."

Brody was still unsure, but the only other option was to head home with his busted bike and cop an ear full from the drunk giant. "Alright," he said. Todd smiled and then punched him hard in the arm; Brody winced.

"That's for running into me," said Todd, "Now we're even."

CHAPTER 4

Brody had never been in a house as big as Zoe's. Although it was the same style as his, there were four bedrooms, two bathrooms and a garage that would have been about the size of most people's homes. He was still not sure if he could trust his three new 'friends', but they seemed surprisingly easy-going.

They headed to the back porch where Zoe placed his bike on a table along with a toolbox. She looked it over like a concerned doctor examining a patient. Todd and Mike both lit cigarettes and watched her in silence.

She began by removing the chain and cleaning the rust off the spokes. Todd offered his cigarette to Brody, who shook his head.

"You don't smoke?" Todd looked completely shocked.

"Um, well, no."

He smiled, "Don't worry, you will."

"Yeah, nothing else to do around here," said Mike as he finished his smoke and immediately lit another one. "What's the diagnosis, Doctor Z?" he asked between puffs.

"Easy fixed," she said, "I'm just going to put this chain from my brother's old bike on it." She oiled the chain and expertly attached it around the spokes.

Brody took a moment to take in the group. Todd was a lot taller than the rest of them, and despite his original threats of a beat down, he seemed quite gentle in his movements. His brown hair was cropped short and he had the lithe build of an athlete. Mike was the complete opposite; about the same height as Brody, his long black hair was a mess and he seemed to be always stooped forward, peering at everything through his mop of hair.

Then there was Zoe; she had long, curly blonde hair, which she'd pulled back in a ponytail. She was short and perhaps even stocky in build, with a pretty face. But it was her eyes that really caught his attention. They were the deepest green he'd ever seen. Brody felt a strange flutter in his stomach; he looked her up and down. His gaze came to rest on her face again, only to find that the deep green eyes were fixed on him. She raised an eyebrow and again he felt the flush of heat to his face.

"Hey, what's ya name again?" Mike was suddenly leaning in and staring intensely at him.

"Brody," he said, leaning away from the smell of cigarettes and sweat.

"Yeah right. Have you been watching that 'Weird or what' show on TV? You know the one with the old Star Trek guy?"

"Ah, no I–"

"Well in this one episode there was this monster called 'Moth man; fully killed heaps of people in this town in America and even made this old bridge collapse and killed a ton of even more people!" Mike chuckled and looked around at the others, "Pretty messed up, right?"

"Mike, what was the point of telling us that?" asked Todd.

"Well it makes you think Toddski, what other things might be creeping around out there? Maybe there's something right here in this house! Like in this other episode, these English people did a séance and called up a demon they couldn't get rid of" Mike chuckled like a cockatoo and suddenly swung around to face Brody. "Fucked up, huh?"

Zoe flicked a rusty washer at mike, which bounced off his head with a light 'ping,' and landed in Brody's lap.

"Shit, Zo'. What the hell was that for?"

"Don't swear!"

"That fucking hurt!"

Zoe hefted a wrench and made to throw it. Mike ducked under the table; she dropped the wrench back in the toolbox. "Made you flinch, Mikey."

"Still bloody hurt!"

"Poor baby. Hey Todd, why don't you grab a beer for yourself and the little lady?" Zoe said.

"What about your dad?"

"He won't notice; he's got tons stashed away. What about you?" The deep green eyes fixed on Brody. "You want one?"

"Um, I don't really drink, sorry. Thanks though."

The others stared at him with varied levels of shock. Mike peered down at him. "So let me get this straight, you don't drink, you don't smoke, what exactly do you do for fun?

"I just don't like drinking, that's all," said Brody.

"Do you wank?" Mike asked, his face deadpan before Todd grabbed him by the shoulders and led him inside.

Zoe had finished attaching the new chain and was slowly spinning the wheel to make sure it was working. Satisfied, she placed the bike on the ground. "Done," she said with a nod.

Brody moved over to examine her handy work. "Where'd you learn this stuff?"

"My brother mainly, but dad was a mechanic before he got into real-estate."

"Will your brother mind that you took his chain?"

She gazed at him for a moment then started packing up the tools. "No, he wouldn't mind."

Both of them were silent as he watched her finish putting the tools away. She pulled her hair out of its ponytail and ran her hands through it. For the third time, he felt that odd flutter in his chest.

The door to the house flew open and Todd tossed a coke into Brody's hands and handed a beer to Zoe. Mike was already half way through his. He put his arm around Brody, and leaned in to cover him in beer and cigarette breath.

"Me and Todd just had a quality idea, you like to ride, right?"

"Um, yeah."

"Have you been to the skate park near St Patrick's high school?"

"No."

"Sweet. We're all going there tomorrow to rip shit…" he stopped and looked at Zoe who frowned at him. "I mean… *stuff* up?" she nodded. "You in?" Mike beamed with anticipation.

Brody was still unsure; but there was something about these guys that seemed different. There was no bullshit, no faking – what you saw was what you got.

"Well, do you want to come or not?" Todd asked.

Brody thought for a second. "Can I ask something?"

"Yeah?"

"Why are you guys doing this?"

"What do you mean?" Mike said.

"Well, like fixing my bike for me, inviting me to hang out. Is this a trick?"

"No, you knob-jockey," laughed Todd. "Look, you're new here and as you've probably noticed, not a lot goes on around the Pastures, even at the best of times. And holidays are worse, so it's good to hang out."

"Yeah," said Zoe. "Besides, you looked kind of, well…"

"Like a loner?" offered Mike. The others glared at him. "What? He does. No offense man, but you do reek of loser."

Brody smiled and flicked the washer that he was still holding at Mike, hitting him square between the eyes.

"Ah, you bastard!"

The others laughed, even Mike. "So," said Todd, "what's your story Brody? How did you end up here, in the asshole of the world?"

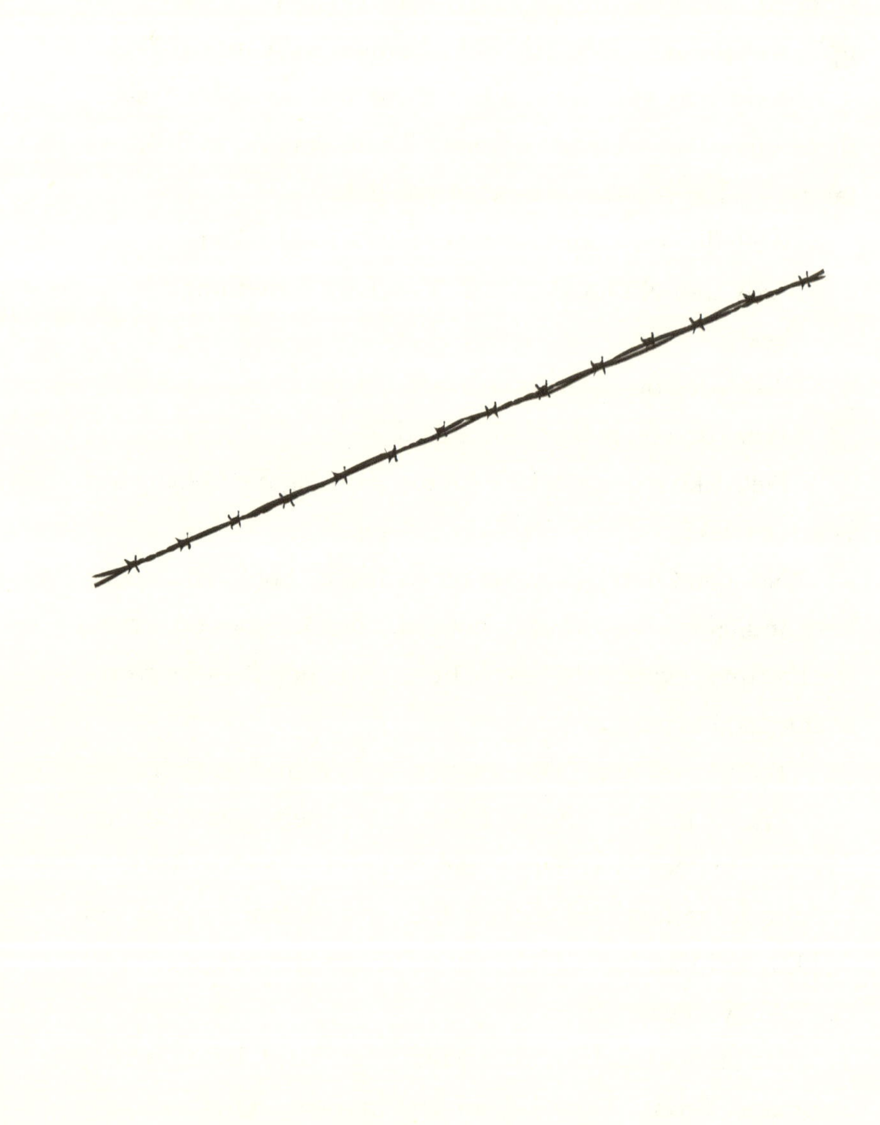

CHAPTER 5

T he sun was almost set when Brody rode home. He took a different route to the one he'd taken with the others. It was longer but it was downhill so he could let the evening breeze wash over him.

He didn't want to go home yet; the giant would still be slumped in front of the TV and his mum wouldn't be home until the early hours of the morning. *Time to explore a little.* The streets of Golden Pastures were as quiet as ever; lights were on in the houses but the evening was silent, almost brooding. Brody peddled past the last few grand houses and into the area of empty plots. The developers had cleared the land and the streets had been laid and paved, but the area was devoid of any dwellings. *Or people.* Only a lone street lamp at a spot where one of the streets abruptly stopped, gave any resistance to the night –a bright island in a sea of dark.

He skidded his bike to a stop and sat himself with his back resting against the cool metal of the lamp. He looked out over the empty plots and past the estate's boundary fence. *Was that the shadow of another building in the distance?* But his thoughts were stuck on the blonde girl with deep pools of green for eyes.

He'd never really felt this way about a girl before; he wasn't even sure exactly what he was feeling. He'd liked other girls of course, but there was something about Zoe he couldn't shake.

She was pretty, but still, a little 'boyish.' But there she sat, in his thoughts, refusing to move. Was he in love?

Ha, don't be stupid; you've only just met her.

He sat for a while allowing himself the simple pleasure of thinking about her. He tried to imagine what it would feel like to have her head resting on his chest, her hair tickling his chin.

A rustle in the trees snapped him back to reality. A possum must be scurrying over the branches. It was making a hell of a racket though. Brody thought he saw something dart from one tree to another, but whatever it was, it moved too fast for him to get a clear look. The possums were out looking for food, which meant it was probably time to head home. Hopefully his dad would be passed out by now. He hopped on his bike and peddled away.

A set of pale eyes watched from the darkness.

CHAPTER 6

Brody parked his bike by the side fence then crept through the back door to the kitchen. He could hear the rhythmic snoring of his father over the din of the television.

His mum often left him a sandwich or cold left-over's for his dinner. But as he'd expected there was nothing but an empty plate and a scrunched up note in the fridge. The giant had got there first. He carefully opened the crumpled note and read his mother's perfect handwriting.

'Won't be home till late, sweets. Here's a little something to keep you going. Love you, Mum. xxx'

Brody quietly closed the fridge door. He padded into the living room where his dad sat slumped in his easy chair. He still wore his work clothes even though there was no work to go to. Brody looked at the man and felt the sinking feeling in his gut again; his dad was starting to look older than his actual years. A hazy image of what he had once been. Brody picked up the slew of empty bottles and takeaway containers that littered the living-room floor. He found some cold chips smothered in thick gravy in a container. He sat at the kitchen table in the dark and picked through the remnants of the giant's meal. That sinking feeling settled in for the night.

CHAPTER 7

Over the next few days Zoe, Todd and Mike showed Brody all the hidden wonders of the Golden Pastures estate –the river, the skate park and the large shopping centre. The days were long and hot, and with their bikes as their only means of transportation the group would always return to Zoe's air conditioned palace in the afternoon to either talk about nothing on the sprawling back veranda, or watch movies in the biggest living room Brody had ever seen.

Zoe's dad had a huge collection of TV shows and movies stored on a hard drive and when the afternoon got too hot the gang would hide in there from the heat.

But Brody didn't watch much of what was on the huge plasma screen; he took the opportunity to watch Zoe instead – to watch the light from the screen cast different shadows across her clear skin. Sometimes the four of them would spend hours talking, Mike always trying to steer the conversation towards his own weird and varied interests – from alien abductions to the government putting mind control chemicals in the water. Mike was odd, but Todd and Zoe kept him under control. It was almost as if the two of them were like his minders. The boy was almost fearless when it came to finding new things for the gang to do, which was how the group found themselves standing in the empty plots of land Brody had discovered a few nights before.

It was a fresh, sunny day. A day Todd had called a "third bowl of porridge, kind of day". The others had all stared blankly at him.

"You know? Not too hot, not too cold; it's just right." The others looked at each other, confused. "You know? Like in Goldilocks and the three bears?" Todd looked around for support while the three snickered and laughed.

"You been reliving your childhood in your spare time, Toddski?" laughed Zoe. "So cute."

"Man, that was lame," giggled Mike.

"Screw you Mike, you virgin," Todd said.

"Well, of course I'm a virgin, and so are you. We're fourteen dickhead, der!"

Todd gave a sly smile; Mike's face sank. "No way! Who?"

"A gentleman never tells."

"You bastard," Mike said pushing Todd.

"He's having you on," said Zoe.

"Am not, Sarah West from Parkside High, at her brother's end-of-year party," he said with a grin.

Zoe flashed a look of disbelief.

"So what are we doing here?" said Brody trying to change the topic.

"Glad you asked, Brodtown. Step this way and I'll show you."

'*Brodtown*' was Mike's new pet name from Brody, and he was desperate to make it stick. Mike led the group towards the boundary fence.

"See that rusty spire over there? Well, the other day I was riding down Patterson Street just over here," he jabbed a thumb over his shoulder, "when I saw it, and it dawned on me that we've never had a close look at what that rusted spire thing actually is and–"

"Isn't it just some old barn or something?" Zoe asked.

"Wait, don't cut me off, I'm building to something," said Mike and Zoe rolled her eyes. "As I was saying, we've all seen that thing poking its head out over the trees, but none of us know what it is. So, last night I was bored and Mum is never around so I went down there and had a look." Mike stopped at an opening in the wire fence and gestured for the others to head through.

"This better be worth it Mikey, I hate going bush," said Todd as he squeezed his tall frame through the fence.

"Trust me, Toddski, you are going to freak when you see this place."

Mike smiled and paced ahead. Suddenly Zoe let out a pained yelp. All the boys turned in unison. Brody found himself running to her before he even knew what was wrong.

"Was it a snake?" Todd asked.

"No I just got my hair caught; like a loser," Zoe said.

"Ha! Fail! It's more than caught, you're tangled pretty badly. I think I can get it out though." Todd said.

"Ouch! Don't pull it!" she winced as he tugged at the

caught strand.

From out of nowhere Mike produced a Stanley knife, and in one swift movement, cut the trapped piece of hair free and continued walking into the bush. "Come on crew, it's not far," he said as if nothing had happened.

"What the hell is he doing with a knife?" said Zoe as she inspected her hair for damage.

"I worry about him," Todd began to inspect her hair as well, "Let me see."

"No, I'm fine. I don't need you fussing over me!"

"What's gotten into you?" he asked.

Zoe glared at him, her eyes flashing bright in the sunlight. "Nothing; come on, let's get this over with," she said as she stomped ahead.

Todd turned to Brody. "That time of the month?" Brody shrugged and walked on.

"Don't *you* start getting moody," said Todd.

The group made their way down the steep hill. Soon the estate was out of sight, the rusty spire getting closer. They came to a stop at a thick clump of blackberries; Mike was beaming mischievously at them. "You ready?" without waiting for an answer he pushed through the blackberry bush. The group followed and stood in awe of what was before them.

They were on the edge of a dusty clearing; the trees towered above them casting deep shadows. Caged in by the clearing, was a house. *No, more than just a house*, thought Brody. *It was a mansion!* Hell, by his standards the place was a castle. But, it was a complete wreck, and any grandeur the house had once possessed was hidden beneath rust and decay. It looked like it should have fallen to pieces years ago. But still it stood, peering down at the group, uncaring and grim.

"Well, fuck me," exclaimed Todd.

"Language," said Zoe.

"This is amazing, I've lived here three years and I've never known about this," Todd said, ignoring her.

"Do you reckon any one lives here?" whispered Brody.

"Nah, it's empty," said Mike as he lit a cigarette before handing the pack and his zippo lighter to Todd."

"How do you know it's empty?" Brody asked.

"Because I went inside last night. Trust me no one's been in there for years."

"You went in *there*?" Zoe was stunned, "At night?"

"Yeah, it's awesome!"

"You weren't scared?" she asked.

"Of what Zo'? It's empty," he exhaled a plume of smoke into the air, "You guys want to check it out?"

"Fuck that!" said Todd.

"Why? Are you scared, Toddski?" Mike said with a smile.

"Mike, don't be a dickhead, I'm not going in there because it's dangerous. We're in the middle of the bush for fuck's sake; there could be snakes or spiders or God knows what. Now come on, let's get out of here." He turned to leave. But Mike calmly strolled toward the house.

"Mike, what are you doing? Come back. What if someone is in there?" Zoe said, her eyes darting to the other boys for support.

"I told you, I looked last night. I can't believe you guys are scared. It's just an old house." Mike continued toward the once-proud dwelling.

Brody took in the dark windows and the rusted roof; despite the fact that it was a warm summer day the whole area was caked in shadow with only pockets of sunlight slipping through the covering canopies. His attention was drawn to one of the ground-floor windows. For a brief moment Brody was sure he'd seen movement behind the glass. It was as if someone had stuck their head round the corner of the window to peer outside then ducked back again.

"Mike, wait!" Brody called. "How do you know there's no one in there? I mean how can you be sure?"

Mike stopped and sighed dramatically; he dropped his smoke on the ground and picked up a large rock. In one smooth movement he hurled the rock as hard as he could. It landed with a clang as it meet the corrugated-iron roof. In the quiet of the bush it sounded like a bomb going off.

Mike turned and smiled at them, "See? Nothing." He ran up to the front door and knocked loudly. "Hello, any ghosts in there?" He laughed and motioned to Todd to throw the zippo over.

Todd did so. "Come on, that's enough, man. Let's go, the place is fucking creepy."

Mike rolled his eyes and pulled a bent cigarette from his pocket ready to light it.

Brody heard the creak of the old heavy door as it swung inwards. Mike swallowed loudly and turned. Peering into the gloom beyond, Brody could just make out the slouched shape of a person – a pair of sinister eyes peered out from the dark, a shudder ran through his body. The Zippo slipped from Mike's hand and landed on the veranda. A pale bearded face slipped from the shadows. The face of an elderly man, eyes blazing with anger, his sunken cheeks and hooked nose gave him the look of a vulture waiting to swoop on its prey.

When he spoke his voice echoed around the clearing. "Who…are you?" The old man intoned.

Mike smiled nervously; Todd took a step in front of Zoe, who sank back behind him.

Only Brody managed to speak, "We're sorry, sir. We didn't know anyone lived here and…"

Mike suddenly turned on his heel, leapt off the veranda and bolted past the others and back up the hill.

"Stop!" the old man yelled.

Brody was about to speak again when Todd's strong hands grabbed him by the arm and pulled him away, "Come on, man. Let's get out of here!" he said.

The three friends scrambled up the hill. Brody glanced back over his shoulder to see the old man calling after them, but his words were drowned out by the wind as they continued to crash up the hill. It was only when they were safely back through the fence that the four of them stopped running and bent over to catch their breath.

"Shit, I gotta cut back on the smokes," said a breathless Mike. The others were staring at him grim faced. "What?"

"You dumb shit. You said the place was empty!" yelled Todd

"It was. I swear it was empty," said Mike.

"Then who's that old guy?"

"I don't know, but I swear he wasn't there last night. We're safe, so what's the problem?

"The problem is, he could have been some crazy fuck with a knife or something!"

"Hey!" yelled Zoe, and the boys spun to look at her. "Watch the language. Now let's just get out of here before he follows us."

A panicked look spread across Mike's face, "Shit, my Zippo; that old bloke has it!"

"So, we'll just buy another lighter from the shops," said Brody.

"No, you don't get it. That zippo belonged to my dad." Mike's eyes were wide, he pulled at his hair as he paced back and forth. "I can't believe I fucking dropped it!"

"Look," said Brody. "Let's just wait for things to calm down; we did throw a rock at his house, so going straight back probably isn't the best idea." He clapped Mike on the shoulder. "We'll go see if we can find it tomorrow, okay?"

Mike stalked back to the street, Brody made to call after him but Zoe shook her head, "I'll talk to him," she said, and jogged ahead to catch up.

CHAPTER 8

The sun was beginning to set as the four friends sat on Zoe's back porch finishing the last of their smokes and beer. Brody still hadn't touched a drop since meeting his new companions but Mike had downed three in a very short space of time. Brody had been unaware Mike had lost his dad; he'd never spoken of it. *He can have mine if he wants.*

Mike suddenly stood. "I'm going."

"You okay?" asked Zoe.

"Yeah… there's just a special about the Roswell UFO crash on the History channel. I don't want to miss it."

"You could watch it my place, mate," said Todd.

"It's all good. I just need some time to chill out," he said and gathered up his wallet and keys. "School starts soon guys, not much of summer left. Maybe I'll see you tomorrow?"

"Mikey." Zoe stopped him with a light touch on the arm. "We'll get it back for you, somehow, I promise."

Mike smiled at her then took the steps to the back yard and disappeared around the corner of the house.

"I didn't know it meant so much to him," said Brody.

"We didn't know him before his dad died," Zoe stated. "It was about a year ago I think. But he was close to him."

"The thing is man, Mike has, well, problems," said Todd.

"Problems?"

"He's a smart guy, knows a lot, but he doesn't really get how to act around people. He kind of just hangs on to us," said Todd. "When I first met him I was walking home and saw these three kids laying into him.

One of them was filming it on his phone, too. I didn't know what it was he'd done, but I ran over and smashed one of them, told them to piss off."

"He even broke the phone on this kid's head," Zoe chimed in.

"Todd smash!" he said, doing his best 'Hulk' impersonation.

"Turned out they were from his school and asked him to come down for a skate, but it was all to make one of those crazy bash-videos for YouTube. You know the ones I mean?"

"I haven't seen anything like that," said Brody.

"Well, they're not pretty that's for sure. Anyway, the point is he trusts people too easily. He's always on the look-out for people to hang with, do crazy shit." Todd paused and took a long swig of his beer. "That's why we hang out with him – he's a good guy but he's not all there, and no one else looks out for him so we do."

They sat quietly for a while; they were an odd mix, it was true – jock, nerd, tomboy, and… well, Brody wasn't sure how he fit in yet.

"Can I ask you guys something?" he said, "That time I ran

into you guys on my bike, how come you invited me to hang out? I mean really." Brody looked from one to the other waiting for an answer.

It was Todd who spoke first. "Because, well…" he gathered his thoughts. "It's not just Mike who's a loner, we all are. That's why we stick together. We look out for each other because no one else does. That's all there is to it man, and when the holidays end and we all go back to our different schools, we'll still be there to look out for each other even though we'll all be far apart. That's just how it is."

Silence fell over the three again. Todd downed the last of his beer and in the soft glow of the porch light he looked older than his fourteen years. "And on that happy note, I'm off."

"You're going?" Zoe couldn't hide her disappointment, but Todd seemed oblivious.

"Yeah, I think I'll swing by Mike's and make sure he didn't go running off to that old house again." He gave her a light peck on the cheek and clapped Brody on the shoulder as he passed him. "I'll give you a call tomorrow."

Zoe and Brody sat quietly while Brody tried desperately to think of something to say to her. He was grateful when she broke the silence.

"He's right, isn't he?"

"About what?"

"Even when I'm away at school in the city, I don't have anyone," she smiled. "Well, anyone close I mean."

Her emerald eyes burned into his but he forced himself to relax. "I didn't know you went to school in the city."

"Yep, my family is always moving but my school stays the same. It's an all-girls' school, very posh. I go back a week after you guys." She continued to stare at him, he wasn't sure if she wanted him to talk to her more or not.

"I better go. It's getting late, my dad's on a real mean streak at the moment. Don't want to piss him off more than he is already."

She stopped him with a light touch to his chest. "I'm glad you crashed into Todd that day." She kissed him lightly on the lips and then walked inside.

Brody would remember that moment for many years to come.

CHAPTER 9

Brody didn't go home straight away; he'd managed to keep contact with the giant down to a bare minimum, and the giant seemed just as happy as Brody about the whole situation.

He only saw his mother briefly in the mornings – when she arrived home from work or late at night if she got off early. Sometimes he thought he heard her standing by his door listening to see if he might be awake. On the rare occasions that she had actually opened the door and softly called to him, he had pretended to be asleep.

Why he did this, he wasn't sure. His family couldn't last the way things were. Something was going to give sooner or later and he didn't want to be there when it did. But he knew fate would make sure he was.

For now, though, he was happy to ride around the estate. He thought about Mike and how a simple lighter could mean so much. Zoe had been right; they had to look out for one another. No one else would.

Brody turned his bike in the direction the empty lots. He was going to get that lighter back.

CHAPTER 10

He would be lying if he'd said he wasn't scared as he pushed his way through the scrub to the clearing. Even though the house wasn't too far from the estate's fence line, the trees surrounding it swallowed what little moonlight there was. The old house creaked as the night wind whistled around it, and Brody wondered how anyone could spend even one night in the terrible old place. Mike must've been either crazy or fearless to go inside by himself.

Probably a little of both. He wished he wasn't alone; even the giant would have been a welcomed companion.

Brody crept to the veranda and began to search for the lighter by running his hand across the rough boards. He checked on the ground in front of the house, then in the few dried bushes that might have once passed for a garden.

After about twenty minutes he was ready to give up, but something pulled him to look inside the house its self. He made his way up to the front door and peered through the dusty windows on either side but it was too dark to see anything. He stole around to the other windows; the wooden boards marked his progress with soft groans. When he had made his way around to a set of large bay windows on the side of the house, Brody found it. The Zippo sat on a dusty dining table, the silver case reflecting the dim glow of the moon. For a long time Brody listened for any sound of movement in the house, but all seemed quiet.

He crept to the back door; it was locked but he noticed that one of the windows was opened a crack. He forced it open about a foot then poked his head in. Before his courage left him, he squeezed himself through the window and crouched beneath the sill.

He was in what must be the kitchen, although the fittings, and cupboards were gone. To his right was the dining room, the Zippo still sparkling in the dim light.

Grab it and go. Do it now! Don't stay any longer then you have to! As quick and as quiet as a mouse, Brody dashed into the room, snatched the Zippo, and made for the window – he'd done it! He just had to climb out and…

"I was wondering if you'd be back."

He spun and was confronted by the hunched shape of a man. "Please," Brody spluttered. "I was only looking for the lighter. I'm not a robber or anything I–"

"Calm down, boy," the old man grumbled. "I'm not gonna hurt you. Hell, I'm too old, should be me who's afraid of you!" he fumbled with something in his hand and then a soft glow warmed the room. It was an old oil lamp. The weak flame fought against the darkness and flickered this way and that before growing stronger.

The old man set it on the floor and folded his arms; he was dressed in a faded overcoat and coarse cotton pants. He had a wild, grey beard that stretched down to his stained, white shirt.

"I wasn't stealing anything, I swear!" Brody could hear the panic in his own voice.

The old man looked Brody over. "What were you kids doing out here? It's not safe to be trekking through the bush you know. People have accidents." The old man leant forward, his face illuminated by the soft glow of the lamp. "They… disappear."

Brody gulped; the old man burst into laughter. "I'm only playing with you, son. What's your name?"

"B-Brody, sir."

"Ah, I see. My name's Pete," he said with a grin.

"Um, nice to meet you," Brody stammered as he extended a shaky hand.

"Are your friends with you?"

"No, I came alone."

"You're brave to come creeping around here at night."

"I just… I just wanted to get Mike's lighter back. I really didn't even think anyone actually lived here."

"I live here! And you lot come down and throw rocks on my roof?"

"We didn't know, really we didn't."

"Ah, that boy, the shabby looking one. He's the one who came creeping through the house the other night." Brody shifted uncomfortably, the old man stared down at him for a few moments. "If that thing is so important to you, take it."

"Thank you, sir," Brody said, edging towards the window.

The old man laughed again, not unkindly, but then his tone changed. He scratched at his chin, his gaze landing on the trees outside. "You should head home now," he said. "It's late; you shouldn't be out here now. Run on home, son."

Brody didn't need to be told twice. He unlocked the back door and headed outside.

"One more thing," said Pete. "You and your friends stay out of the bush. I mean it when I say it's not safe here, do you understand?"

"I'll tell them, sir," said Brody with a nod.

"Good. Now hurry along boy!"

Brody jogged off towards the dim glow of the distant estate and glanced over his shoulder when he heard the old man speak.

"So, here we go again."

CHAPTER 11

The others were skimming stones on the lake when Brody caught up with them the following day. The weather was warm and the sun shone brightly, however, the gang seemed glum. The holidays continued to roll on and relaxation had given way to boredom.

Todd and Mike were swigging beer, an opened six-pack at their feet. Zoe was lighting three cigarettes at the same time. When she saw Brody approach she lit a fourth and then handed them round.

Brody allowed himself a brief glance at her, taking in the green eyes that seemed to him to sparkle even brighter than the clear water of the lake. "I've got a surprise," he said, breaking the silence.

"Keep it in your pants, buddy," Todd said. "Otherwise I'll have to take mine out and then Zoe will faint."

"Shut up." Zoe hit him hard in the shoulder.

"Ah! Easy, crazy bitch!"

Zoe hit him again.

"What is it, man?" Mike asked flatly.

Brody held out the lighter. Mike's eyes lit up and his jaw hit the ground. But…how?"

Brody smiled as his friend took the Zippo and turned it around in his hands. "Well… I went into the house," he said.

"Get out!" said Todd, giving him a playful shove. "Did you run into the old fella?"

"Yeah, he snuck up on me, too. I totally shat myself," Brody said; the boys laughed but Zoe had the worried-mother look she sometimes liked to wear.

"So, what happened? Did you have to do a runner?" asked Mike as he all but jumped on the spot.

"No. He was cool, but he told me to tell you guys that we shouldn't go down there anymore."

"To the house?" Zoe asked.

"No…well yeah, but he meant don't go into the bush," said Brody, "He says it's not safe."

Todd pressed a beer into Brody's hand. "You're one crazy freak, buddy, but I like it."

Brody held the beer but didn't open it. Zoe's big greens were staring at him; he felt his cheeks flushing. Was she going to jump forward and plant a kiss on his red cheeks for being so brave? Or maybe even on the lips!

"That was a stupid thing to do," she said softly.

His heart sank.

"You shouldn't have gone there by yourself." She dragged on the smoke before flicking it into the lake.

"And the award for biggest killjoy goes to…" Todd hooked a thumb at her.

Mike suddenly leapt forward and gripped Brody in a bear hug, "I love you, Brody! I think you've turned me, dude!" He planted a wet kiss right on Brody's lips. "I want the world to know it; I love Brody Webb," he shouted.

Todd howled with laughter. "Hey, let's get some more beer and head over to mine. The folks are at some dinner thing tonight," said Todd then he and Mike raced off towards the shops.

Zoe followed, while Brody walked beside her in silence.

Say something idiot, don't walk the whole way there without saying anything!

"So…" he began. "Why are you dark on me? I just wanted to…"

"I know, just tell us at least. We're supposed to look out for each other, remember?"

She took the beer from his hand, popped it and drank deeply. They strolled in silence as up ahead Todd and Mike were chasing and wrestling each other.

"How are they going to buy more booze?" He asked, desperate to keep what little conversation they had going.

"I gave them my brother's ID card. Todd looks a bit like him, shorter hair though."

"Won't your brother mind?"

"No, he wouldn't mind," she said glancing down at him.

"Where is your brother?" he asked, "Has he got his own place, or something?"

She looked thoughtfully at him. "We used to live in New South Wales, near Penrith. He told mum he was going for a bike ride in the bush."

He felt a flutter in his stomach; he'd opened an old wound.

"But really he'd gone off drinking with his friends. They crashed on the way back and he died." She looked like she had more to say but instead she stepped up her pace.

Smooth mate, really smooth.

CHAPTER 12

The following day, a council worker found some shoes and a backpack a few metres inside the boundary fence of the estate. There would have been nothing too strange about this, except that a wallet inside the pack belonged to a Martin Thomas – the same Martin Thomas that had been missing for almost a month. Police swarmed the area in the hope of finding him alive – at least that was what they said – but in reality they were looking for poor Martin's body.

For a few days, Brody and his friends watched on, as the Golden Pastures estate swarmed with activity. Rescue teams, helicopters and emergency services buzzed about the bush looking busy.

But they found nothing, not a trace of him. Only his shoes and his backpack gave any hint as to what may have happened. The police only said that their investigations were on-going and they were now suspecting foul play.

So, after a while the news crews disappeared, and the search teams dwindled until only a few bits of scattered police crime-scene tape showed that anyone had come at all.

The new school term was drawing closer. Brody didn't want things to change; he'd never had friends like these and it was as close to feeling happy as he'd ever been. Still, his mother trudged off to work with the world sitting on her shoulders and the giant cocooned himself inside the house. Brody was hardly ever there, except for a few days when Zoe and Todd both had family gatherings to attend. He'd tried hanging with Mike but the kid was a handful.

So rather than tempt the giant's wrath, he'd take his bike and ride. He did laps of the estate and would always find himself at the vacant lots, the rustic turret of the house poking over the trees. He wondered if Pete was still there. There was only one way to find out. But something about the way the trees seemed so still at night, made him heed the old man's advice, to stay out of the bush.

CHAPTER 13

I t was after one of the hottest days on record that Brody got the fright of his life. The sun was setting and the cool breeze blowing down from the mountains had brought some much-needed relief. All down his street people had thrown open their windows to let the cool change blow through. There was a strong smell of barbeque, and every now and then there would be a burst of laughter from his neighbour's house.

He was doing his best to clean the kitchen, because his dad had promised him a 'clip around the ear' if it wasn't done by the time he got back from the bottle shop. He was almost done when there was a knock at the door.

He wiped his hands on his t-shirt and walked to the door. When he opened it, he had to stop himself from slamming the front door and sprinting out the back.

Zoe stood on the steps, her hair was tied back in a tight ponytail and she wore a lose singlet and cut off denim shorts. She clutched a laptop to her chest and smiled brightly when she saw him. Brody was terrified; he'd never wanted any of his new friends to see his house, especially in its current state. But he held his panic in check as best he could.

"Hey!" he said, way too loudly.

"Hi. Sorry to just drop in on you, but I didn't know your home number," she said.

"That's cool. Um, what's up?" Brody said, still too loudly.

"Well, I was wondering if I could show you something. I was going to get the others to come too, but Todd is at a family thing and Mike has a doctor's appointment or something. Which is a shame, he loves this sort of stuff," she tapped the laptop.

"Yeah, great," he nodded.

She smiled and shifted from side to side. Even though the silence only lasted a moment it felt to Brody like and age. "So…" he said. "What is it?"

"Um… are you going to let me in?"

It was only then that he realised the screen door was still shut. *Dickhead.* "Shit, sorry."

She smiled knowingly as he unlocked the screen door and ushered her in.

He set them up in the kitchen, seeing as it was the most respectable looking room in the house. He also made sure the doors to the other rooms were shut to keep the smell of stale beer and cigarettes out. He opened the back door to let the breeze flow through.

"How'd you know where to find me?" he asked as she set up the computer.

"Easy, I just looked you up on line. There was an old number for this house but it's disconnected, and like I said, I don't know your new one so I thought I'd just drop around. You don't mind, do you?"

"No, course not, it's just a bit unexpected."

She sat in front of the computer and started opening up a bunch of files. "I couldn't find you on Facebook, or Insta either."

"I'm not… I don't have Facebook."

"What's your wireless password?"

"Huh?"

"For the 'net."

"Um…"

"You don't have the net? Like, at all?" She looked concerned more than anything else. "How do you do homework and stuff?"

"I just do it in the library at school."

She turned back to the computer and he felt his cheeks flush, but this time it wasn't from the embarrassment of having her catch him looking her over. It was from the simple realisation of how little he had.

"Here we go," Zoe said, breaking him out of his thoughts. Have a look at this," she said and turned the computer towards him.

On the screen was a series of newspaper stories, which she scrolled through.

"What is it?" he asked.

"When they found that guy's stuff near the boundary fence, I went over to watch the cops searching. I overheard one of them saying something like 'he's not the first.' It got me wondering what they were on about."

"I did some digging on the net, and downloaded all this last night." She said, as she tapped a few keys and one of the clippings filled the screen. It looked old, slightly yellowed. Brody read the headline out loud: "Family of three missing in bushland." She hit some more keys and another one of the clippings filled the screen.

"Hikers go missing in national park," he read. "So you're saying this has happened before?"

"Yep, quite a few times." She scrolled through the many clippings; her face had donned that concerned-mother look. "I went through a whole bunch of news and history sites and found all these reports of people going missing in the area. It stretches right back to like the 1920s."

"And no one's ever noticed this?" he said. "It might not be anything weird though, I mean people going missing *is* strange, but it's the bush, people get lost all the time, and not just around here."

"True, but there was something else." She scrolled to the beginning of the clippings. "Look. 1928… 1942… 1956 and so on."

"So?"

"Well, they're all fourteen years apart. Every fourteen years people go missing – no trace ever found." She smiled. "As Mikey would say: 'pretty messed up, huh?'"

"Yeah, you were right."

"About what?"

"He *would* love this."

"Yeah. Wait until we show him – he'll lose his mind."

They shared a chuckle but then Zoe went quiet, her chin resting on her hand as she scrolled back and forth through the clippings. "The really weird thing is they never find them, only their stuff. It's like they drop everything and just walk into the bush."

"We need to show Todd and Mike. Maybe the old guy at the house could tell us more," Brody said.

"Are you kidding? I'm not going anywhere near the bush, not after all this," said Zoe, waving her hand at the screen. "Didn't that old guy say not to go there? Now we know why, right?"

"Don't you want to find out more?"

"Well, yeah. But it just sounds… I don't know… spooky."

"You've never struck me as a girl who freaks out easily," he said.

She crossed her arms and turned the big greens on him. "Hey, I'm not scared! Well, it's pretty creepy, but whatever's going on out there I don't won't to get too close to it." She turned back to the computer. "Besides, what could we do? Surely the cops would know about this already. They obviously don't want too many other people finding out though."

She started tapping away on the keys again. "Oh, there was this one story. Here it is. Someone was found after being missing for like two weeks." She brought up a small newspaper article and read it aloud: "'Found walking naked and disoriented ten kilometres from his last known location' but they don't give his name."

Zoe sat back chewing her lip, then grabbed his arm. Brody smiled at her touch.

"Oh, and it goes on to say they could never get a proper word out of him about what had happened. He just went on and on about, 'things in the bush whispering to him'. He spent the rest of his life in a mental hospital somewhere."

She let go of his arm and continued scrolling through the clippings; Brody's skin tingled where she'd touched him.

"What's your e-mail? I'll send it all to you." She looked up at him, Brody shrugged. "Serious? You don't even have an e-mail?"

"I've never needed one. Besides I can't afford… we don't have a computer."

"At my school it's compulsory. We have to…"

"Yeah well, clearly I don't go to a flash school like you, alright?" He hadn't meant for it to come out as harsh as it did, and he saw the shock written on her face.

"I didn't mean it like that…"

"I'm sorry, I shouldn't have said that." He ran a hand through his hair; there was a long, awkward silence before he continued. "You guys are all great; you're the best friends I've ever had, but I go over to your houses and you've got everything you could ever want then I come back to this shithole and what do I have? Nothing. A fucking rusty bike, and an old man who hates me, and I don't even know why. I never did anything to him!"

She closed the laptop and stood; she was going to leave. He couldn't blame her; why should she care? But instead she leant against the kitchen bench and pushed a loose strand of hair from her face.

"You know how I go to boarding school in the city, right?" He nodded. "Well the truth is, it was my idea."

"Why?"

"I don't like staying with my parents; I don't like coming home. For me, home is school. How bad is that?"

"But why?"

"Ever since my brother died they haven't been the same. It's like they never got over it, you know? Not like it's something that you just get over." She shrugged, a hopeless gesture. "When he died my dad pretty much buried himself in his work; that's why he's so successful – he never does anything else. He's always away or getting home late. My mum's the same. That's why I've got all this sort of stuff," she tapped the laptop. "They think it keeps me happy."

She let out a long breath before continuing. "I hear Mum crying some nights, and other nights I see my dad just standing in front of the picture of my brother in his office. Sometimes he's smiling, but most of the time he just stares."

She looked at him, her eyes were watering, but she flashed him a faint smile before looking away again. Brody thought she had never looked so beautiful as she did in that one small moment.

"It feels like they don't want me around, so I decided that I wouldn't be. It's like they forgot that I lost someone too, sometimes I wonder if they wish I'd–"

"Don't say that," he cut in. "You know it isn't true."

"Do I?"

He sighed. "I guess not." He reached out and took her hand. "What was his name?"

"Andy," she said with a smile. "He would've liked you."

For a moment the only sound was the distant rustle of wind through the trees and the laughter from his neighbour's backyard.

"Look, my old man will be home soon. We should walk back to your place," he said letting her hand slide from his.

"No," she said as she sat down and opened the laptop. "First, I'm going to set up an e-mail for you and then I'm going to put you on Facebook. It's time you entered the twenty-first century."

"But I don't even have a computer," he said. "What's the point?"

"Your neighbour's wi-fi isn't locked, so I can use that for now. And you can use your school's computers when you go back."

Brody was so rapt to have one-on-one time with her, he forgot all about the giant's imminent return. It was dark when he heard the creak of the back screen door and the heavy boots clomping through the laundry.

The giant swayed in the doorway; it was clear he'd stopped at the pub instead of the bottle shop. There were some screwed-up betting tickets in his hand and, as always, he was accompanied by the smell of stale beer and sweat.

"Good news kiddo!" he boomed. "I won seventy bucks on the trots." He hadn't registered Zoe yet.

"I lost about fifty, but still came away with a win." He suddenly took a shaky step back and turned to face Zoe. She smiled uncertainly and he swung back to look at his son.

"Who the fuck's this?"

"Dad, this is my friend Zoe. She lives over on–"

"Since when did you man up and get a girl?"

"Dad, please."

"Nah, it's all good!" He regarded Zoe, a sly smile etching its way onto his face. "Shit, Brody, if I was thirty years younger I'd have a crack meself!"

"Dad, just go watch telly or something. Please."

"It's okay." Zoe closed her laptop and stood. "I should go. My parents will wonder where I've got to."

"Nah, hang about love, I want to know what the little fella did to get you over here." The giant moved to block the door and Zoe's big greens turned to Brody, unsure. "So tell me, how did he pick up a nice piece like you?"

Zoe stood straight and looked the giant in the eye. "I better go Mr Webb. It was nice to meet you, I'll see you round Brody," she turned and headed to the front door.

The giant eyed her as she walked out. "Another woman walking out on us, hey mate. Bloody typical!"

"Dad!"

"You could walk me home," Zoe said over her shoulder. "If you want."

"No he can't. He's got work to do, like cleaning this fucking mess." He waved a hand around the spotless kitchen. "So just piss off, will ya?"

Zoe turned and walked away, her shoes making a soft patter down the front driveway.

"She's cute. Not really my type, but I'll be happy to take her off your hands, mate," said the giant then bellowed with laughter.

Brody regarded this stranger who had once been his father. He was unshaven and his hair had the sheen of grease from not being washed in a while. Something in the big man's appearance made the boy pity him, and while he felt the swell of anger and frustration, he knew there was no point in fighting him. The only thing his old man cared about was from where the next drink was coming from.

His father was rummaging in the fridge; he pulled out a half-empty bottle of beer. "What you reckon, mate – half-empty or half-full?" The bottle slipped from his hand and smashed on the tiled floor. "Fuck! Grab something and clean that up will ya?"

"No." Brody couldn't believe what'd he'd just said. Butterflies started fluttering in his stomach as the giant turned to him, his expression hardening.

"What? I don't think I heard you properly, boy."

"I said no!" The butterflies were fluttering like crazy now. "It's your mess; you clean it up."

The giant looked stunned. Brody took his opportunity and made to walk out of the kitchen. A strong, rough hand gripped his shoulder and turned him around.

"I'm not cleaning it, Dad. You made the–"

The slap came hard and without warning. One second

Brody was standing, the next he was lying on the cold tiles. Those same rough hands wrapped around Brody's neck and yanked him to his feet. Held almost off the ground, he was face to face with his blustering father.

"You don't fucking talk to me like that, do you understand? I worked my arse off to get this fucking house and you spit it back in my face!"

Fighting off the spinning in his head, Brody pushed his hands hard into his old man's face. But it had no effect.

"Do you know how hard I worked for you? Know what it's like to work like a dog ya whole life and then be treated like one? You don't even give a shit. No one gives a shit!"

Brody was suddenly in flight but only for a second. His back met the fridge door with a hard jolt.

Father and son stared at each other. The big man was breathing heavily, his face flushed with rage. Brody pushed to his feet, using the table to hold onto. Slowly his father's expression softened, the anger replaced by shock.

"Shit, mate... I'm sorry. I didn't mean to," he said, reaching out a quivering hand. "Are you all right?"

Brody bolted out the back door. He heard the heavy boots of his father as he gave chase. Brody grabbed his bike as he ran, jumped on and pedalled harder then he'd ever had.

Behind him the slurred calls of the giant grew softer and softer until they were replaced by the sound of the rushing wind as it whipped about him.

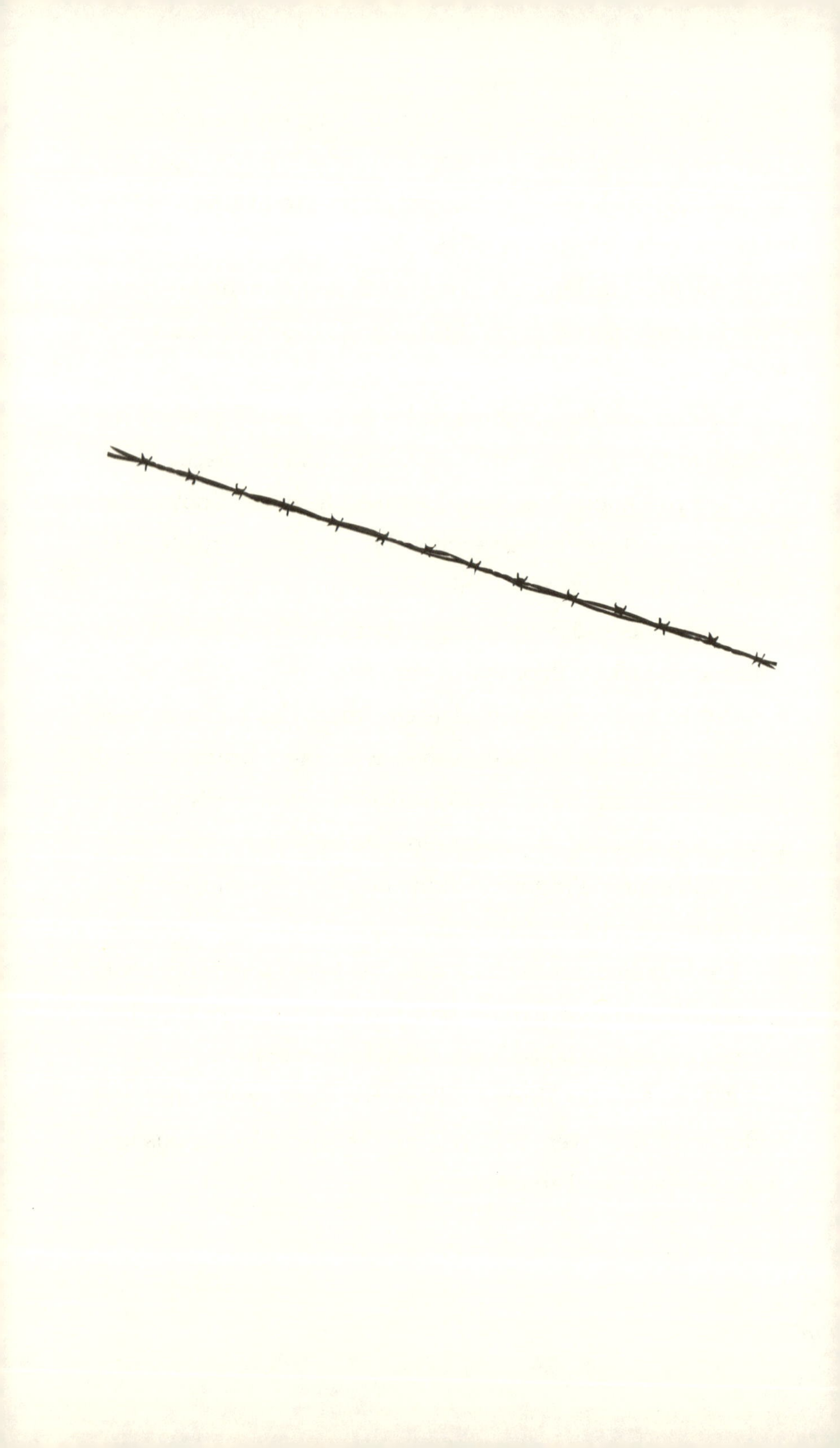

CHAPTER 14

He rode to the only place he could think of – the empty lots. He dumped his bike in the long grass and walked as far from the solitary street lamp as he could. He wanted to be in the dark for a while; he wanted to let his tears fall. He was tired of holding them in.

He wouldn't go home tonight. He'd sleep here if he had to; the night was warm enough. Sure, he'd have to go home sometime, but not tonight. His tears were not from pain, but anger; an anger that was turning into hatred for the giant.

If I were bigger I'd kill him. I would. I'd kill him. I'd… He shook his head. *Dad, what happened to you?*

The tears eventually ceased and he curled up to sleep. The wind rustled through the trees and the tall grass swished back and forth, gentle and soothing. He was not sure how long he slept when a distant scraping caused him to stir.

The sound came again. Closer. The street lamp cast more shadows than it rid. *Plenty of places for someone to hide.* When the scraping came again, he sat up and scanned the area. Maybe it was some homeless person, or even some of the older kids that lived around the estate. But he could see nothing.

There. Again. A… soft, slithering. Brody started to make his way over to his bike. He tried to be silent but the grass betrayed him with every step.

Even though he could not see any real threat, the air seemed charged with energy. The night had suddenly grown still. Even the trees beyond the fence line were silent, as if poised to up their roots and run.

Then he saw it.

The tall grass shifted one way then the other, as if some invisible person were walking toward him. But… it wasn't invisible, it was crawling.

He ran for his bike but the thing changed direction and cut him off. The shifting grass was the only thing that gave it away.

Brody tried to switch direction, but it anticipated him and scuttled to cut him off again.

He stopped, his heart pumping with adrenaline. Just what the hell was this thing? A loud grunt from the grass silenced Brody's thoughts and he shivered in the warm night. The thing slithered forward. At speed!

Brody sprinted toward the boundary fence and hurled himself over. As he tumbled down the hill in the dark he heard the heavy breathing of the thing as it closed in.

Branches scratched his face and arms as he stumbled deeper into the bush. He crashed forward and smashed into a huge gumtree; the breath knocked clean out of him. Branches snapped. Close. Closer.

He didn't see the thing but its warm breath tickled his

ear and the grass brushed his skin as it slithered around him. Brody held himself tight and closed his eyes waiting for the final attack.

Nothing. The thing was still there; its laboured breathing sent plumes of dust into the air. Brody forced his eyes open, and could just make out the strange shape of the thing. It retreated a few feet, hissing angrily, and he rolled over to see what had distressed it.

The hunched figure of a man. "Get behind me, boy. Now!" The man's voice cut through the night air like a blade, causing the creature to hiss again.

Brody did as he was told and crawled towards the figure. He spotted the outline of the old house against the trees and realised where he'd ended up.

The man stepped forward and the creature spat and hissed as it retreated. "So, they're sending the dogs to do the hunt for them?" the man said, as he kicked dust at the thing. "Have your masters become so weak they don't dare step out of hiding anymore?"

The thing let out a nervous grunt as it cowered before him.

"You remember me, don't you little one?" Brody could hear the smile in the man's voice. "And so do your masters." The man knelt before it. "Remember the last time? When I escaped…" he trailed off as a deep rumbling sound rocked the earth around them.

The man and the creature both turned to the bushland. The thing slithered away as the rumbling came again.

The man stood, his eyes never leaving the dark outline

of the trees that surrounded the clearing. "I want you to very slowly stand up and walk to the house. The front door is open. Close it behind you," he said.

"Please, what's happening?"

"Do it!" the man commanded. "And don't turn your back on the bush."

Brody scurried backwards toward the house, stumbled up the steps to the veranda and through the door, slamming it shut. Inside he peered through one of the dusty windows. The thing in the bush eclipsed all his fears of the old house.

He watched as the man cautiously stepped to the edge of the clearing. "Are you there?" he called. "You remember me, don't you?"

His call was met by silence.

"You will not take this boy, do you understand?"

Silence.

"I will not let you!"

Silence.

"Show yourself, you cowards!"

A deep, resonant groan shook the house; the widows cracked and one even shattered, showering Brody in shards of glass.

The sound droned on. Brody peered through the now broken window; strange shapes danced in the dark beyond the clearing. The man stood with his hands in the air, palms spread as if warding the things back into the void.

Suddenly, another rumble shook the house. The sound of glass breaking came from somewhere up stairs. Then silence.

He thought he could hear whispers, soft and calming. They seemed to be coming from everywhere. The man stepped back and peered into the scrub.

"I do not fear you," he stated.

Something grunted and slithered away into the night; the sound of trees cracking and falling marked its progress. Whatever it was, it had been big…*very* big.

Brody closed his eyes; desperate to believe it had all been a dream when he suddenly realised the old man was crouched beside him. He had not heard him enter..

"Are you alright, lad?"

"Pete?" he whispered; it hadn't sounded like the old man outside.

"That's right, I'm sorry you saw all that," he said. "Come on, let's get you home."

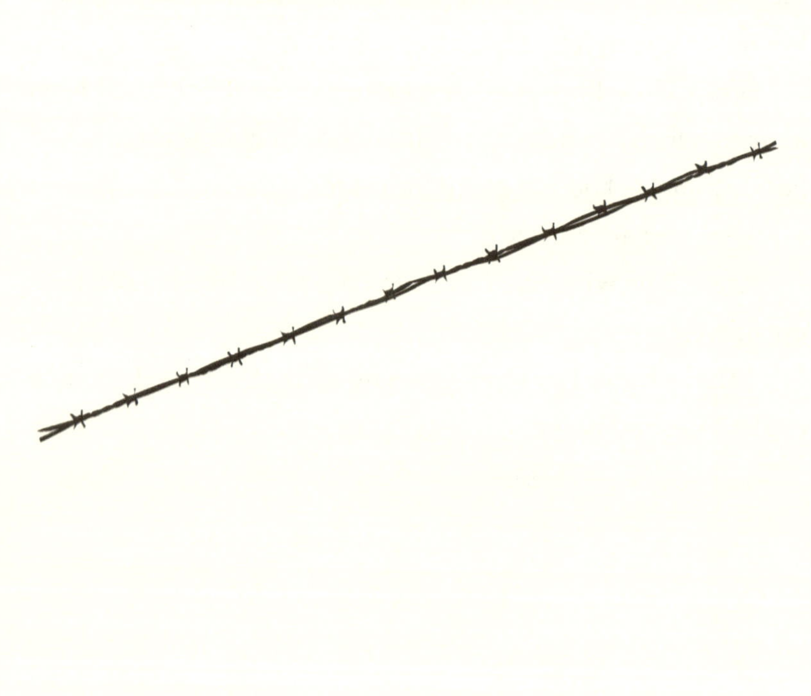

CHAPTER 15

It took a while for Pete to convince Brody that it was safe to make the trek back to the estate. But the old man led him safely through the trees and up the steep slope to the boundary fence. He found the hole they had used the first time they'd come down to the house, and stepped back into the inviting glow of the street lamp.

"I suppose you want some answers, don't you?" Pete said. "I meant what I said; I'm sorry you went through that but I told you to stay away. Why is it that kids never take notice?"

"I didn't," he protested. "I was here and it chased me!"

Pete bit down on his bottom lip. "I've never heard of one going out in the open like that. They must be getting desperate." He turned to look out at the black expanse of the bush. "And to think I dared to hope it was over."

"What are you talking about?"

Pete looked down at Brody, his rough hands stroking his beard thoughtfully. "We're not alone."

"No shit!"

Pete chuckled at that. "The thing that chased you tonight

is a sort of scout. It weeds out prey – you were just in the wrong place at the wrong time." He returned his attention to the swaying trees. "I'm worried though. They never pass the fence-line. Even before the fence was there, they never came out this far."

"We better tell the cops. If these things come out again-"

"Police? Ha! The same police who just spent two weeks searching the bush for that poor hiker? Tell me, what did they find? Nothing, that's what, and they never would." Pete lowered his voice; his eyes held Brody to the spot. "They are the bush, you see? You could be standing right next to one and never see it until it wants you to."

"I thought I was going to be… I was so scared."

"Who wouldn't be?" Pete said. "These things are old, but they've gotten weak. Trust me boy, this will pass. They will come out from their hiding places, take what they need and then be gone again. But you need to make sure that you and your friends stay away from the bush. Don't even come here," he waved a hand to indicate the vacant lots. "They have ways of getting to people, make them enter of their own free will. Don't give them the chance. Do you understand me? They hate us for building on their home, and they use us for…well, never mind about that."

"Building on their home?"

"You think these estates were always here? No, this was their place long before we stuck the fence up and called it ours," Pete said. Then his wrinkled face softened. "You better get home, lad."

"But what about you? You can't go back in there, not after…"

"It's all right, the house is…safe for me." He turned and headed for the fence line.

Brody watched the frail old man as the darkness closed in around him. "How do you know so much about these things, what are they?"

"Better you don't know," Pete called back.

Brody had no intention of staying in the vacant lots alone; the giant at home paled in comparison to the twisting shadows he'd seen that night. He untangled his bike from the thick grass and cycled away into the welcoming glow of the street lamps.

CHAPTER 16

Despite the comforting warmth of the sun in the clear-blue sky above, Todd felt strangely uneasy. He walked quickly through the empty streets, his long skinny legs striding across the footpath. He carried a shopping bag packed with junk food and his faded football. The estate was always quiet, but for a perfect day like this, it was bizarre that no one was outside. He turned off the empty streets and decided to take the short cut across the oval.

The rusty goal posts came into view on the far side of the field. Todd dropped his bag and began to jog towards them, bouncing his ball as he went.

He couldn't wait for the start of the footy season; Saturday's filled with a match in the afternoon, drinks with the boys after, and then off to whatever parties were going on that night. And the girls… wow! How could he forget them?

The private school he attended made a big deal of football – a lot of league players had come through the ranks, and Todd hoped he'd do the same. He slowed at the fifty-metre line, his lungs burning for air. Too many smokes and beers; he'd let himself go these holidays, but that would change. He'd hit the gym this weekend and start getting into shape.

He was going to miss his crazy friends when the holidays were over. They were a weird bunch, but they were the only real friends he had. Sad but true. Zoe had been in his thoughts more and more. He thought it strange that the girl he'd scabbed a smoke from at the shops once had become such a big part of his life. They had nothing in common other than living in the same area. He'd miss her the most; the way she tried to be so mature and keep them all in line. She must be the only girl he'd never heard swear, and the fact she hated it so much was endlessly amusing to him. He liked her. A lot. But if they only saw each other during the holidays, how would that work out?

Todd lined up for a kick at goal, imagining the roar of the crowd. His foot connected perfectly with the ball, and he watched with a smile as it sailed between the posts before bouncing into the bushes.

"Still got it," he said to himself.

The imaginary roar of the crowd died away, replaced by the rustling of the wind through the trees. He walked over to where the ball lay beneath a tangle of weeds and shrubs and reached under. His hand scraped the leather and he tried to knock it toward him but it wouldn't move. He lay down on his stomach and reached in again. Hooking his hand around the ball he dragged it out, but as he did something dry and rough scraped against the back of his hand. *Snake!* his mind screamed. He grabbed the ball and stumbled back from the bush, scanning the area for any sign of the snake, but there was nothing.

Unnerved, he hurried back to the oval but stopped, scouring the ground. His bag was gone. How could someone have taken it without him seeing? He'd only turned away for a minute.

If someone had run past and grabbed it, he would have seen them. The feeling of unease grew, and standing there in the bright sunshine he suddenly felt very vulnerable.

The rustling of the wind through the trees was the only sound. But when Todd looked to the bush that encircled the end of the oval he realised there was no wind. *If it isn't the wind making the trees rustle…*

Whispers. They held him to the spot. The ball fell to the ground and he suddenly had the overwhelming urge to walk into the bush, even though every part of him screamed to run for the houses. But the urge was too strong, and Todd found himself turning and walking toward the tall swaying trees. In the undergrowth a strange shape squirmed back to the shadows. Though most of him was paralysed, his feet continued to walk him into the bush.

Then everything hushed. The only sound the crunch of Todd's shoes on dried leaves as he walked deeper and deeper into the bush. But soon that died away.

Silence.

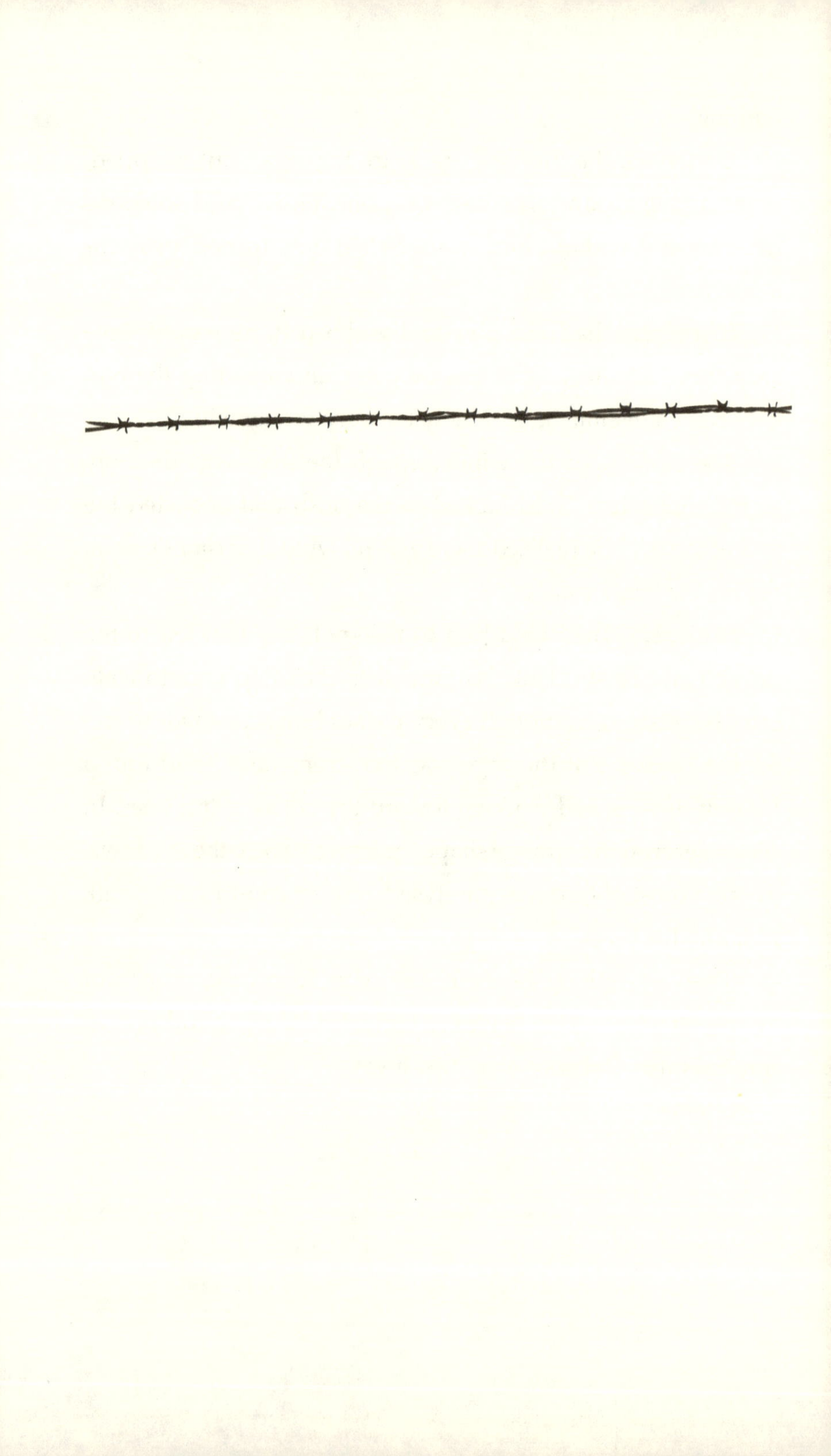

CHAPTER 17

rody was still amazed at how good Zoe was with fixing things. She had set up his bike, which she had affectionately named 'Rusty', on the driveway. He'd had to break into his old man's shed to liberate the tools needed but another clip around the ears seemed a small price to pay to have both a working bike and spend time with Miss Green Eyes.

After his run-in with the...well, whatever it had been the other night, he was glad to have her there in the bright sunshine. He was still weighing up whether he should tell her about what had happened when she broke his thoughts.

"You sure your dad won't get angry?" she asked, casting a glance toward the house.

"He'll never know. He's gone off to the pub anyway and won't be back until dark." Brody felt more relaxed around her now, but he could tell she wasn't happy about being in the giant's territory.

"I'm sorry about the other night," he said. "My dad, I mean. He's got… problems."

"Ha! Yeah, I think your dad and my dad should hangout," she said. "Pass me the wrench… not that one, the small one." She pulled off a rusted washer and threw it behind her before turning her attention to the deflated tyres. She pulled one off the spokes and held it up. "See this?" she said, poking a finger through the shredded hole in the rubber. "Too many skids. You'll blow your tyres every time."

"Can you fix it?"

"Not here, you'll have to bring it round to my place sometime,"

"I don't do that many skids, the tyres are just shit."

"Language! There's a lady here." She looked at the grime on her hands. "Not that you'd know it."

"Zoe…"

"Yeah?"

"Would you want to… you know… see a movie or something?"

"At my place you mean?"

"No, I mean…" The butterflies were back with vengeance, and he steeled himself as best he could; the big greens were looking at him uncertainly. "I mean, would you want to go out…with me?"

She seemed taken aback, unsure if he was serious or not.

"I mean you might be busy or something so it's no big deal if–"

"I'd love to–"

"Really?"

"Yeah, but–"

She was cut off by the sound of a car horn tooting. His mother's old hatchback pulled up just in front of them and she stepped out and waved to the pair. She was wearing her faded factory uniform and her hair was tied up in a bun, but she shouldn't have been home this early. His mother looked from him to Zoe then gave her son a faint smile.

"Hi guys," she said. "What are you up to?"

"Hey Mum, Zoe was just helping me with Rusty," he said indicating the old bike.

His mother examined the mess on the driveway. "Didn't know you were good with fixing stuff, Brody." She mussed his hair and he felt his cheeks start to redden.

"Mum, stop." He tried to flatten his hair back into place but the damage was done. "Zoe fixed it all, except the tyres, they're stuffed."

His mum nodded. "Nice to finally meet you Zoe. Brody has told me all about you and your friends."

"Nice to meet you too, Mrs Webb," Zoe replied with her best private school smile.

"Does your dad know you've got his tools?"

"No, but I'll put them back."

The smile dropped from his mother's face and was replaced by that anxious look she often wore. "Well, you should do it now, you know what he's like," she chided.

"But Mum..."

"Zoe, would you mind if I take the big man for a bit? Just

got some family stuff to talk to him about. He can pop over later if you like," his mother said.

"Of course! Was nice to meet you, Mrs Webb. I'll see you later, Brody." She smiled, picked up her bag and trotted down the drive.

When Zoe was out of ear-shot his mother turned and beamed at her son, "You didn't tell me she was so pretty! Is she your girlfriend?"

"No! Well, I mean she's a girl and she's my friend, so that kind of counts…right?"

His mother laughed and put her arm around him. "Come inside, sweetheart, I've got something to tell you."

<hr>

Once inside she sat him down in the kitchen and set about making herself a cup of tea. She kept her back to him, but he didn't need to see her face to know that she was weighing up how to break some news to him. It would be bad news; it was always bad news.

"Sweetheart…" Here it came. "I was laid-off today from work," she said. A light steam drifted from her tea cup and was lost in the streaming sunlight of the kitchen window.

"Does that mean you don't have a job anymore?" he said softly.

He watched as she rummaged through the cupboards, pulled out an old tin of Milo and spooned a few clumps into a cup. Anything to keep herself busy, he thought.

"Yes, but it's not all bad. The husband of a lady I work with, has offered me a job at his pub – the one near the supermarket. Pay's pretty good, too. Night work of course. The company even gave me a payout of a month's wage." She smiled at him thinly. "You want a Milo?"

"No thanks," he said, but she poured water and milk into the drink and set it in front of him anyway.

She slumped in the chair opposite, letting her wiry hair free and rubbing the back of her neck. She looked old, he thought, really old.

"Look, big man, I think you're old enough to understand how things are. When your dad and I bought this place it was supposed to be a new start but it hasn't gone to plan has it?"

She sipped the tea again, her brow furrowed in thought. "Brody, I spoke to your uncle Justin last week. You remember him? He lives in Adelaide. He's the one who drives the trucks. Remember he used to take you and your cousins around in them? Remember your cousins?"

"I remember them," he said, that weight settling in his stomach.

"Well, he's opened his own company and he needs help running his new depot. He's offered me a job in the office. It's a good job, sweetie. We won't be rich, but we'll be pretty well off. We'll be able to get you some new clothes and–"

"But we live here. I'm about to start school soon."

"Well, yeah, we'd have to move again, but this time it'll be permanent, I promise."

"Mum, I've just made new friends," he said. "What about Dad?"

She went silent but her look said it all –the giant wasn't part of the plan. "Your father needs to get well. He's not been himself since he lost his job and…"

Brody ran to his room. His mother called after him but he slammed the door and locked it. For a while she knocked on the door, her soft voice trying to coerce him out, but he didn't really hear her. He was going to have to start all over again.

It didn't matter that he'd made his first real friends in years. He felt like breaking something but what good would it do? Most of his things were broken already.

There was a knock at the front door and Brody prayed it wasn't one of his friends. His mother called him again, and this time her voice sounded odd, almost afraid.

Brody, opened the door and was about to call out but was confronted by his mother and another lady. She was wringing her hands, her face a mask of panic.

"Brody, this is Mrs Masters, your friend Todd's mum she–"

"I need you to be honest, Brody," Todd's mother said. "Do you know where Todd is?"

Brody was taken back for a moment; he was still reeling from his mother's news. "Well, I haven't seen him…" he stammered.

"Do you know where he is?" she repeated, as her hands gripped him by the shoulders.

"No. Last time I saw him was like… a day ago, I think."

The two women looked at each other. "Are you sure Brody?" his mum asked.

"Yes. Why? What's going on?"

"Todd's gone," said Mrs Masters, more to herself than anyone else, "He's gone!"

CHAPTER 18

They sat on the floor of Zoe's huge living room. Brody's gaze shifted between his two friends; Mike was rocking slightly, although he looked calm enough. Zoe, on the other hand, was a knot of worry. She'd tried ringing Todd a dozen times but the calls had gone through to his cheerful message bank.

'Hey, you've called Todd, leave a message and if I can be fucked' then the sound of him and some mates giggling before the 'beep.'

Finally she'd put the phone down between the three of them and they stared at in silence.

"You reckon this has got to do with…you know, all that stuff on your computer?" Mike asked.

"I don't know," she replied.

"So what do we do?"

"I don't know!" she repeated.

"We should go look for him."

"The cops are already doing that."

"Well, we can't just sit here." Mike was suddenly on his

feet, the Zippo in his hand. He sparked it as he walked around the room.

"Zoe's right," said Brody. "The cops are out there, they'll find him."

"We should show them the stuff that Zoe found, all those clippings and stuff."

"But what good's it going to do? To them we're just kids; they're not going to listen to us. Besides, I still think they know more then they let on," she said, her eyes never leaving her phone.

"So we just sit here while Todd is out there alone?" Mike was all but yelling.

"Keep your voice down, my mum's asleep," Zoe hissed.

"I bet that creepy old guy had something to do with it. He looks like a complete pedo," Mike said, twisting his mouth in disgust. "So we really aren't going to do anything?"

Brody tried to think of something reassuring to say, but no words came to him. Even though he knew something they didn't.

"Todd wouldn't just sit here if one of us was missing, he'd be out there searching day and night. He'd be trekking through the bush no matter how dangerous it is."

"It's worse than you think," Brody said quietly.

"What do you mean?" Mike asked.

Brody told them all about what had happened the night after Zoe had met his dad in all the giant's drunken glory; about the slithering creature in the grass, and how Pete had come to the rescue. And of that terrible sound of the thing in the bushes.

His friends stared at him incredulously.

"Are you messing with us?" Zoe said. "Because if you are–"

"No, why would I?"

Mike scratched his chin. "What did these things look like?"

"I don't know, I didn't really see them,"

"So you didn't see anything?" Zoe looked unconvinced.

"Well, not exactly, but I'm telling you there was something out there. It chased me and–"

"If you're lying to us Brody–"

"I'm not lying!" he said, holding her gaze, "I was… I thought I was going to die."

"And Todd's out there." Mike was pacing around the cavernous living room again. "We've got to do something!"

"But what?" Brody asked. "We can't tell the cops they're not going to believe us, and our parents…" He trailed off as Zoe stood; the big greens looked very focused.

"If Todd is out there, we have to find him. He'd do the same for any of us. If no one else can help us, then we have to help ourselves. We'll go to this Pete and see what he knows."

"Every minute we wait is one minute longer Todd is stuck out there Zo', we should go now!" Mike said.

"No, if these things are anything like Brody says, there's no way we're doing anything until we know more."

Brody looked to his friends and the decision passed silently between them.

"Sneak out tonight and meet at the empty lots. We go together or not at all," she said,

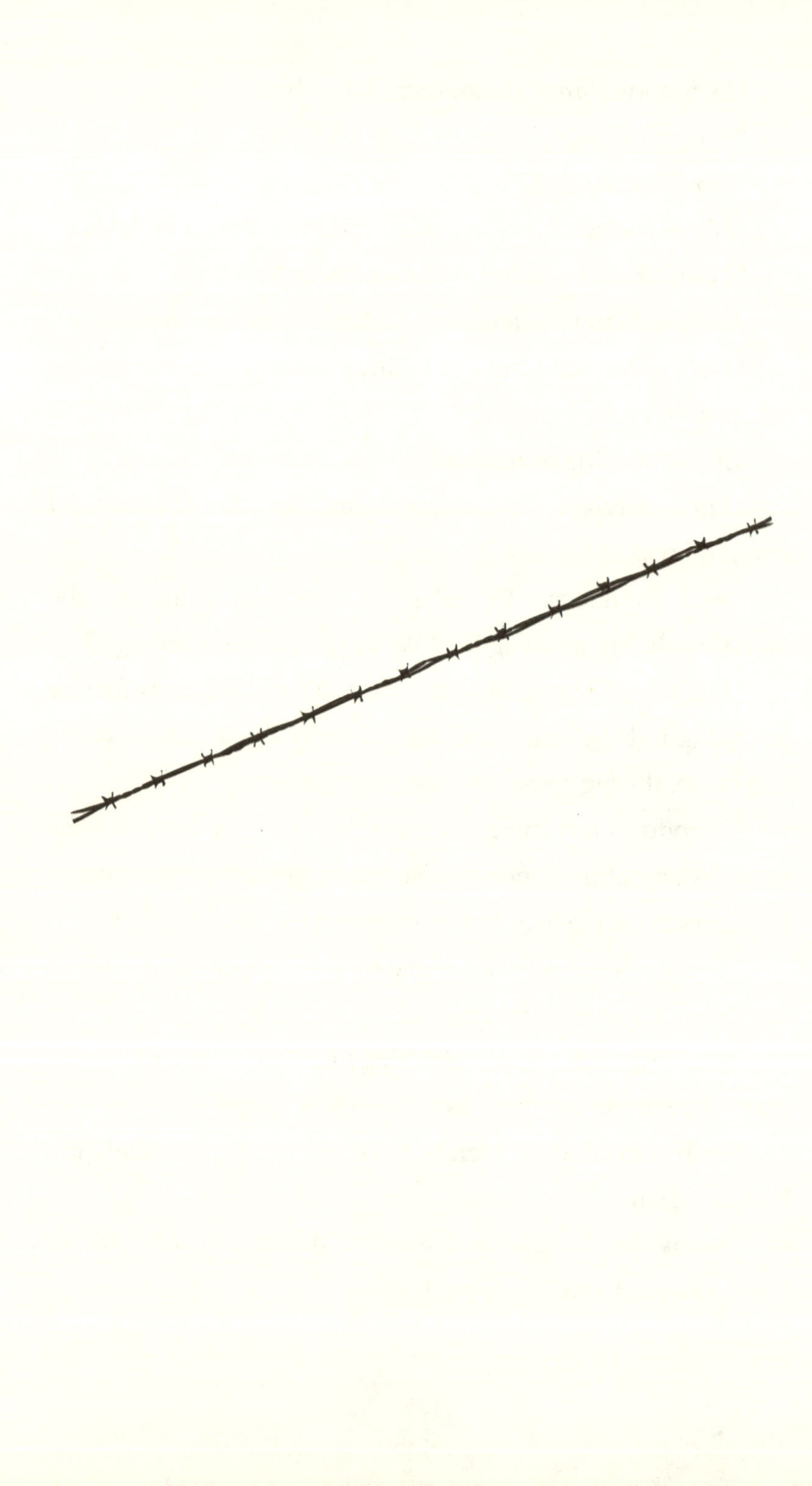

CHAPTER 19

The night was one of the most pleasant Brody had ever seen. Grey, puffy clouds drifted high above, and the cool mountain wind tickled his neck. However, he soon forgot the nice weather, as he walked towards the dark void that was the empty lots. As he rounded the last row of occupied houses he saw Mike pacing beneath the street lamp, a lit cigarette in hand.

"Where's Zo'?" Brody called as he approached.

"She shouldn't be far off," Mike said. His hands were shaking slightly despite the warm night.

"You all right?" Brody asked.

"Yeah." He took one last long drag on the smoke and dropped it on the ground, stomping it out almost angrily.

For a while the two boys stood in silence, both of their gazes stuck firmly on the dark swaying trees beyond the fence.

The whiz of bike wheels had both turn. Zoe cruised to a stop alongside them. She nodded, then chained her bike to the streetlight. Dressed in shorts and a dark hoodie, she could've worn a potato sack, and Brody would have still thought she looked beautiful.

"I hope we find him," said Brody.

Mike let out a long breath and the trees seemed to sway toward them. "We better."

"First things first," Zoe said and stalked off into the dark.

The boys hurried to catch up.

No one spoke as they carefully made their way through the bush to the house. The old building's turret stood out against the cloudy sky like a black beacon. They moved as quickly as they could; every sound filled them with dread. Finally, they made it to the clearing then scurried to the front door like frightened mice and huddled together, searching the shadows for any sign of danger. It seemed funny to Brody that they had once been afraid of the house, and now it seemed like their only protection.

"What now?" Mike whispered, his eyes scanning the darkness beyond the bushes.

Brody pressed his face to one of the hall windows. "I can't see anyone in there, should we call out?"

Zoe stepped forward and banged three times on the ancient door. The sound echoed through the house for longer than seemed possible, but eventually the latch clicked and the door creaked open.

"P-Pete? Are you there?" Brody asked the void. A familiar, withered face peered from the black.

"What did I tell you about coming down here?"

"We need your help," said Zoe.

"I know," the old man sighed, and stepped aside to let them in. "I've been expecting you."

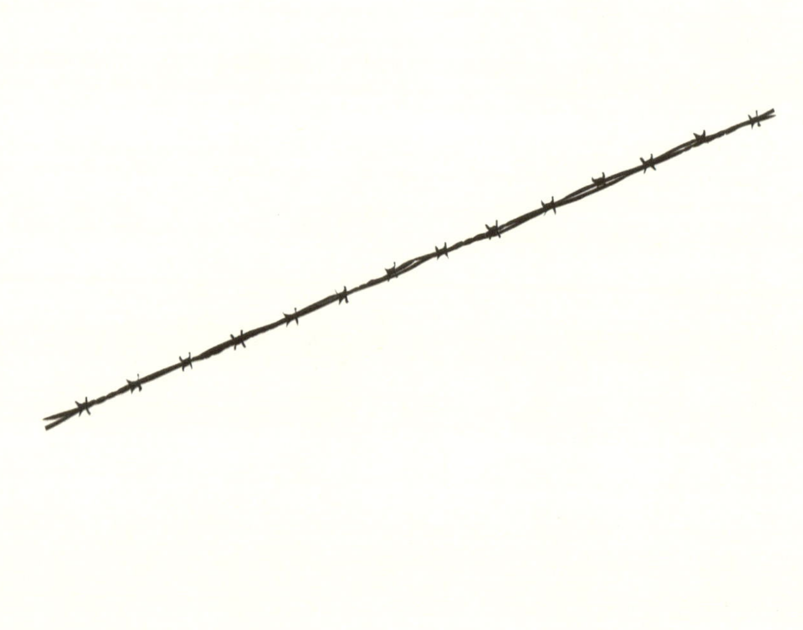

CHAPTER 20

Pete took them through the shadowy dwelling to the dining room where they sat on creaky chairs. The moon shone brightest here, but Pete insisted on keeping to the dark. His eyes lay fixed on the bushland, so it was Brody who broke the silence.

"Our friend disappeared and–"

"Your friend was taken, son," Pete said.

"What do you mean?" Zoe demanded.

"He knows what I mean," Pete said, indicating Brody. "He got a front-row seat the other night didn't you?"

Brody nodded; the memory of being chased by the slithering creature had kept him awake every night since.

"So this thing that chased Brody took Todd?" Zoe was interrogating rather than questioning, but the old man was calm and simply nodded.

"So tell us how we get him back," she continued.

"You can't–"

"Don't tell me that, I've lost someone before and I'm– "

"You're not going to let that happen again, I understand.

But there is something *you* need to understand," Pete said leaning into the pale moonlight. "These are not just stupid animals, they didn't drag him kicking and screaming, they are cunning and powerful. They don't live in the bush, they are the bush."

Mike gulped.

"You really think they didn't see you as you came here tonight? My dear, you would have walked right passed them and not have suspected a thing. They want you here. They want you to come looking."

"But the police searched the whole area looking for Todd," Brody said..

"Like I said, they're smart. They'd rather go up against three brave, but foolish children than a company of armed men." He returned his gaze to the bushland outside the window. "They're somewhere out there now, watching us, waiting."

"He's just trying to scare us," Zoe said. "Who are you anyway?"

"I'm someone who can help," he replied.

"An old freak hiding out in the bush? She said. "Maybe we should tell the cops about *you*."

"I'm not your enemy, love," he said. "You said you'd lost someone before, someone close. I've lost people too, and I've tried, God how I've tried to stop these things. But every time I think they're gone, every bloody time, they come back!" He looked at each one of them in turn as he spoke. "I've asked you and I've warned you, now I'm telling you – stay away from the bush!"

"But Todd…" Mike started to say but Pete's glare silenced him.

"There may not be as many of them as there once was but that doesn't mean they aren't dangerous. If ever you needed to trust someone then trust me when I say your friend is gone."

"So we do nothing?" Zoe said incredulously.

"No," said Pete. "You make sure that none of your other friends come down here, you understand?"

"We don't have any other friends!" said Mike.

"Todd is like a brother, would you leave your brother out there?" Zoe looked a foot taller when she spoke. Her big greens seemed to flash bright in the gloom. "And we *will* get him back!"

Pete sat back in his chair, his voice soft when he spoke. "This is not a game. These things won't just kill you they'll use you, they'll do terrible…terrible things…"

Zoe narrowed her eyes at him. "So there's a chance he's still alive?" She stood. "Where can we find him? Tell us where."

"Please love, you don't know what you're asking me to do. You mustn't go after him. They'll take you too!"

"Just tell us!" shouted Mike.

The old man slumped in his chair his head in his hands. "I don't know where exactly, but if you head to the centre, the exact centre of the bush…" He looked at each of them in turn, a strange look of acceptance written on his face. "They'll find you."

CHAPTER 21

The three friends hurried back through the streets of the estate. Mike lit a cigarette then offered the pack to the others but they shook their heads. They walked silently, the only sound, the *click, click, click,* of Zoe's bike as she walked it along the road.

They arrived at Mike's house, while similar to Zoe's it seemed slightly bigger, if that was possible.

"Mum's still not home," he said. "You guys could hang out for a while if you want."

"We need to rest, and so do you," said Zoe. "Make sure all the doors and windows are locked before you go to sleep."

They weren't scared, they were terrified; everything within them said not to go beyond the boundary fence. Hadn't the old man said as much over and over again? But they were Todd's friends, his real friends. The uncertainty, the not knowing, it was all too much.

"We've got to try, we've just got to," said Brody.

"I'll steal my knife back off Mum," Mike said. "And if one of these things tries it on with us, I'll stab it right in the face!"

Mike mimed a stabbing motion at Zoe.

"I worry about you sometimes," she said with a weary laugh. Then she stepped forward and hugged him. "Get some rest, big man."

They waited for Mike to disappear into his house before Brody walked Zoe home. She didn't say much but when they were standing at her door a thought popped into his head. "What were you going to say the other day?"

"Huh?"

"The other day, when I asked if you wanted to see a movie or something. You said 'I'd love to…but,' what were you going to say?" he asked.

She looked down at her hands, her long hair covering her face. "I was going to say, well, I don't know exactly what I was going to say." She laughed nervously. "I'm bad at this," she said and looked uneasy as she tried to answer him.

Way to make it awkward idiot. "You know," he said, "you're the first girl I've ever asked out."

She smiled at that. "Well, you're the first guy to ask me out."

"Really?"

She nodded.

"But…" he prompted.

"But… there's someone else…and… I couldn't," she said softly. "You know what I mean?"

"Todd?"

She nodded.

"I thought so." He gave her a half smile and made to walk

away. But her hand on his shoulder stopped him; she kissed him gently on the cheek unlocked the door and went inside.

He cut a lonely figure as he walked the last few streets home. The lights of the city shimmered in the distance; so many people so far away. He looked over the houses with their well-kept lawns and four-wheel drives parked out the front. Why was Golden Pastures so quiet?

It was as if people knew, not directly, but deep down they knew something was not right here. The estate should never have been built so close to the bush. The realisation made him shiver, a cold sweat spreading down his back. He thought of Todd, alone somewhere out there.

Please…let us find him.

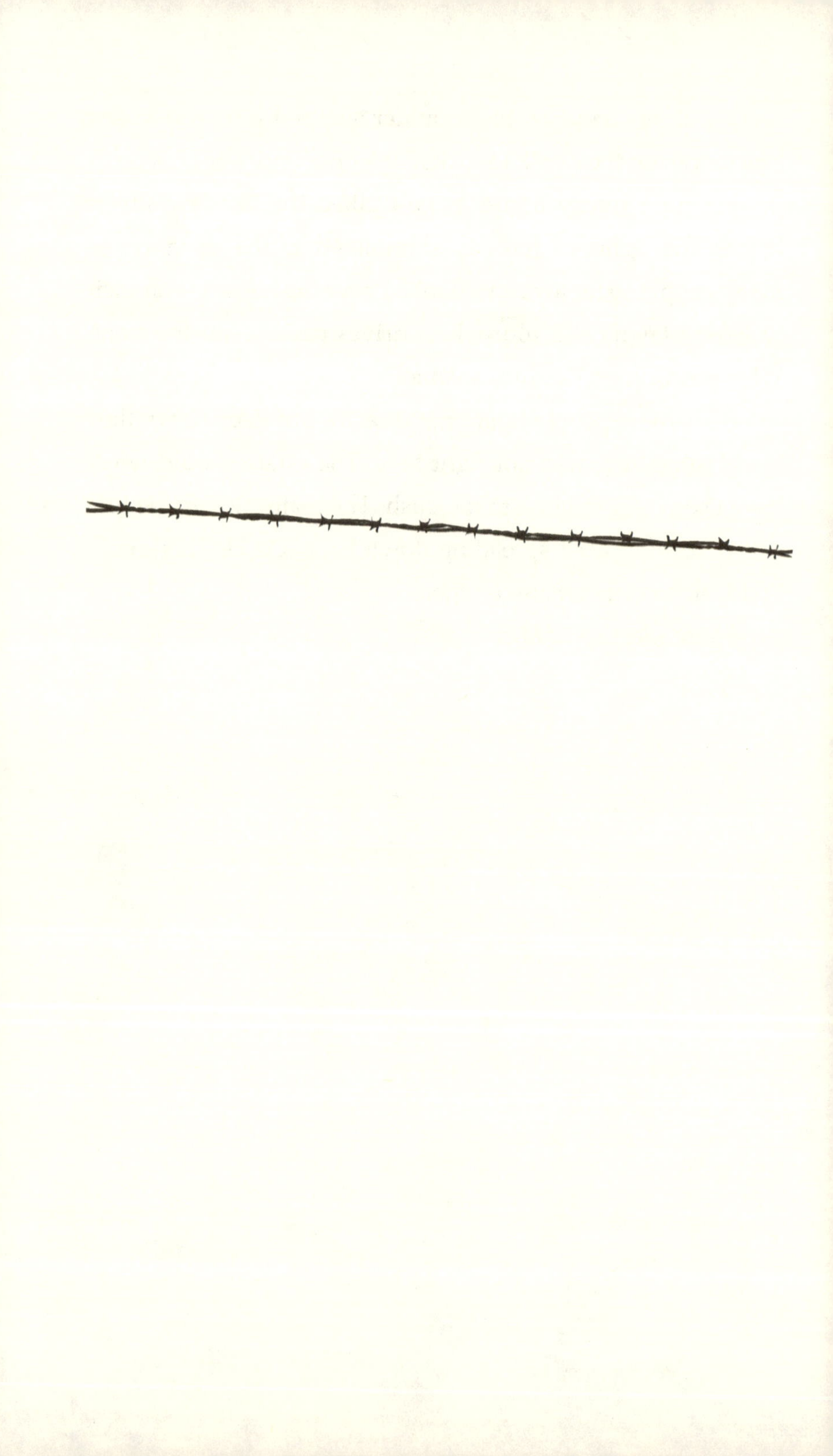

CHAPTER 22

oe slipped off her shoes and padded down the hall toward the grand staircase that led to the second floor. Being careful to avoid the steps that creaked, she made her way to the landing. A soft light spilled through a crack in the door to her father's study.

She peered through, careful not to make a sound. He was sitting at his desk with his back to her but she could see what he was holding – the picture of her brother Andy, the one of him at the mechanic shop he'd worked at. Her father was still in his suit from work; as tall as he was wide, it strained around the man's bulk.

She heard the soft sniffle and realised he was crying, she was about to speak, but instead she closed the door and crept to her bedroom.

She sat down at her desk and flicked on her laptop, it booted to life and she had to franticly drop the volume. She listened for the sound of her parents approaching but all was quiet. She opened the browser to Google maps and punched in the street closest to the bush. A street-view of the estate appeared on the screen and Zoe scrolled out and over to the empty plots and the bush beyond.

'The exact centre of the bush, and they'll find you.'

That could be anywhere! The estate was on the very edge before you got to the real bushland, and then it seemed to expand in every direction. Zoe sat back in her chair; her head was aching and her mind wouldn't focus.

A flutter of panic rose through her; how could they find Todd in all that? It was like trying to find a needle in a thousand haystacks. Her eyes landed on her phone; she tapped it and the screen lit up to reveal a picture of her and Todd. Mike had taken that photo ages ago, and Todd's face was only half in shot, but his hand took up most of the picture – his middle finger extended.

She touched the screen, tears began to well in her eyes. Why had she never told him how she felt? Had she expected some sort of fairy tale where Todd would come riding in on his white stallion and sweep her off her feet?

"I'm going to lose you too, aren't I?" she said to the picture. The screen saver disappeared as the phone went to sleep. She should be saving her energy too; she'd need her rest if she were going to go blundering through the bush tomorrow to try and find 'the exact centre'.

It was impossible. They would never… She suddenly sat up in her seat. Maybe they didn't have to find the exact centre. Maybe they just had to get as close as they could. Maybe, if they waited and saw one of these things they could follow it. An idea was forming in her head; if only she wasn't so tired, she would have it. Wait, maybe she did, perhaps she was over thinking this.

'The exact centre.'

She zoomed out on the image of the map; the bush was vast but it did have its limits. First there was the boundary fence to the estate, then the highway that ran back to the city. There was a dried up stream that wound its way down from the mountains and curved its way past the estate and the highway. She printed out the image, cringing at the harsh noise her printer made.

"Zoe?" Her dad's tired voice called softly from the landing.

She pulled the paper from the printer, and placed it face down on the desk. "Yeah?" she called back.

"What are you doing? It's late. Your mum's got an early start."

"Sorry, just printing out something for school."

"Well, keep it down, all right?"

"Sorry."

"Just keep it down." She heard him sigh; he was trying to build up the courage to come in.

She felt more then heard him turn away. "Dad!"

"Yeah?"

"I love you." She waited for a response, she could almost see him there on the landing, head down, wanting to say something, but unsure of what the right thing to say was. "Goodnight," she said softly, when it was clear he was stuck for words.

"Night, sweetie," he whispered. His soft footfalls

disappeared down the hall to her parents' room.

After a moment she turned back to the map and marked out the farthest points on the boundary fence, the river and the highway. She then joined the dots, making a triangle. *No wonder they called it triangulating.* She used her ruler to find the centre point of the triangle.

Not the exact centre, but it was as close as they were going to get. If they entered through the fence line and headed true west they would get there. It was going to be one hell of a walk though.

She dropped onto her bed, the map clutched to her chest. As she drifted off something else Pete said poked at her thoughts.

"They want you to come looking."

CHAPTER 23

Brody watched from the window as the giant threw his duffle bag into the back of his friend's utility truck. *Funny how someone's whole life can fit into one bag.* He could tell his old man was suffering from a hangover; his lips were dry and cracked, his eyes still bloodshot.

Brody's mother leant against the open front door, a mug of tea steaming in her hand. The giant turned to her. "Please Christie, let's talk about this. You can't just kick me out!"

"That's exactly what I'm doing. I warned you."

"Why are you being such a bitch?" the giant said. "You know how tough things have been for me."

"You don't think it's been tough for me?" she said. "Do you have any idea how hard I've worked to keep us afloat?"

"I busted my arse to get us this house!"

"And I busted *my* arse so we could keep it!"

They stood staring at each other but it was the giant who looked away first. "So that's it then?" he said. "Just like that we're done, are we? After all we've been through?"

"After everything you've put us through you mean."

"For fuck's sake, Christie!"

She stalked toward him. "You hurt our child!" she hissed. "Your own son! You go away and you think about that."

"I was pissed. I… I didn't mean to. Let me speak to him at least," he pleaded.

"Just go, Daniel."

He turned away, catching Brody's eye as he went. He paused as if to say something but a look of defeat slid over him and he jumped into the passenger side of the utility.

The truck sped off into the mid-morning sun and Brody let the curtain fall back into place. The giant was gone but that sinking feeling still sat in his stomach.

He found his mother in the kitchen making yet another cup of tea. She smiled when he walked in; she looked tired but there was a new spark in her eye.

"Are you okay, Mum?"

She nodded.

"When will Dad be back?"

"I don't know, sweetie." She sipped here tea. "We might not see him for a while."

His hand went to the bump on the back of his head, a reminder of his tussle with the giant.

"You're a brave boy," she said with a thin smile.

"I don't feel brave. I feel scared…all the time," he said.

"But you keep going, that's what being brave is – you're scared but you keep going. Always remember that, always be brave," she replied.

He nodded, and for a moment they sat in silence together.

"I'm working a double-shift at the pub today," his mother finally said. "Will you be okay? I could drop you at your friend's place if you like."

"It's okay, I was thinking I might just stay here tonight," said Brody.

"We'll be okay, Brody, I promise you," she said.

He'd heard that before, all those months ago as he'd jumped in the back of the family's old hatchback and begun the long journey out to Golden Pastures Estate. He nodded and forced a smile.

"Well, I better get ready for work, big man." She abandoned her tea and headed for the bedroom. "It might be an idea to start packing some of your stuff tonight, and can you find your school's number for me too? I need to–"

The harsh buzzing of her mobile phone cut her off and she took it from the bench. "Hello? Yes, speaking, yes sorry, I didn't recognise the number." There was a long pause as she listened and suddenly she looked up at her son; she was about to speak but bit down on her lip.

"I see. Are they sure? Jesus… yes, thank you I'll…I'll take care of it, thanks for telling us…well, yes, I suppose you're right, at least he'll get some closure."

She ended the call then faced her son and he knew before she spoke what had happened.

"Brody, that was the officer we spoke to about Todd. Um…" She composed herself. "Sweetie, I'm so sorry. They found a… they found someone in the bush…it's your friend–"

"They found Todd?"

"Yes but…"

"He's…dead?"

She nodded and quickly moved to hug him. Brody felt like the air had been sucked out of him. He felt numb and suddenly very weak as his mother held him.

They had failed before they'd even begun.

CHAPTER 24

Mike's room was overflowing with dirty clothes, random bits and pieces he'd brought home from his many late night, hard-rubbish pick-ups and, of course, dozens upon dozens of CDs and DVDs. He'd cleared a small space in the centre of the room near his unmade bed.

He sat, looking down at his phone as he scrolled through the many photos of him and his friends. He was not a popular kid; he didn't have lots of friends, but the ones he did have were the best he could ever of hoped for.

Sure they teased him sometimes, and they were never interested in hearing about his favourite shows, nor did they ever let him play his music when they hung out. "That's not music, it's just screaming," complained Zoe. Like she could talk. All that pop crap she played hardly qualified as music.

He'd been glad when Brody appeared on the scene, weirdo that he was, it had been great to get someone who would listen to his ramblings. He knew Brody found him weird, but he found Brody weird too, so at least they could be mutually weird together.

It was a change from watching Zoe and Todd trying *not* to hook up. He'd wished they'd just pash each other and get it over with, not that there was much chance of that now.

But now the big Toddski was gone.

He thought about that for a moment, his friend wasn't a friend anymore; he was a memory.

He stopped scrolling through the photos, and threw the phone on the bed. He switched off the light and stood by the door listening to the din of the TV in the living room. He heard the soft snoring of his old lady. She was out, on the dot of midnight, just like every other night.

At least he still had the old lady. She wasn't around much, what with her commute to work every day. She'd had Christmas off last year, not that they'd done anything.

Mike slumped on his bed and reached under the bedside table. He found the bag of weed and the small silver pipe in its hiding spot. He stuffed the pipe, probably a bit too full, and went to the open window.

The night was warm but not unpleasant. He lit the pipe with his father's Zippo and inhaled deeply.

This one's for you Toddski.

He looked out over the well-kept back lawn to the wooden fence and the bush beyond.

The police had all but given up searching the bush when they had stumbled upon the body of Todd. His mum had tried to hide the news reports from him. But he read one on the net that had said, "The body was so disfigured as to be unrecognisable, but what there was left of it seemed to match the description of Todd." The news had said that the police believed it was likely that Todd had met with "foul play".

They don't know the half of it.

The things in the bush had killed him. Tears welled in his heavy eyes; he felt so helpless. He'd thought about ringing Zoe but she might need a little space, and Brody didn't have a phone.

He took another puff of his pipe and felt the light tingling feeling go through his body. He sent a plume of smoke out the window and watched as the breeze carried it over the back fence.

A light rustle of the bushes behind the fence caught his attention. He listened. His eyes strained against the darkness. Something scratched against the fence. It sounded like claws trying to get a hold of the wood. Mike's chest tightened; was it the smoke? He stifled a cough and concentrated on the area from where the scraping seemed to be coming.

In the shadows, something hunched and black scampered onto the fence. Mike watched as the shadow moved silently across the top of the fence before dropping with a soft thud onto the back lawn.

He composed himself long enough to reach for the flashlight he kept next to his desk, and aimed it at the shadow on the lawn before flicking the light on. The beam pierced the darkness and landed on… the biggest possum Mike had ever seen.

For long moments the possum stared at him with disinterest, his heart was smashing against his ribs. The possum hopped away and Mike took a long pull on the pipe before chucking it aside; he shouldn't smoke the strong stuff, it made him jumpy.

He swung himself back on to the bed, slid beneath the covers and turned to look out the window. From where his bed was positioned he had the perfect view of the back yard.

Everything was still.

Another shadow passed across the lawn.

Stupid possums.

He was dropping into sleep when another, much larger shadow passed by his window. Had he seen that or was he dreaming?

Then the shadow returned and stood at the window. Mike sat up and regarded it through heavy eyes.

I'm dreaming, he thought. *It's not real.*

But then the shadow spoke, and the dream became horribly real.

CHAPTER 25

Zoe was not sure how long the phone had been ringing, but the harsh buzzing had continued until she found herself answering with a mumbled "Huh?" Mike had sounded so terrified, that she had snuck out of the house to meet him immediately. She found him under the street light outside his house, cigarette burning away in his shaking hand.

She had to hold him by the shoulders to stop his trembling. He muttered his story about the shadow and how it had spoken to him, telling him of the pain his friend was in – the never-ending dark they kept him in. If she hadn't been through everything she had so far she would have thought him crazy.

"But they found his body," she said, trying to calm him.

"It told me that was another, some… hiker they 'used up', and that Todd would end up the same if we don't help him. Then…then it…" he stammered, "it laughed at me."

"Did your mum hear it?"

"No, it laughed…in my head. That's how it talked. In my head!"

Zoe took her quivering friend by the hand and began to lead him away, but Mike pulled back.

"What're you doing?" Mike asked.

"We need to get Brody and get going now," she said. "We can't leave Todd if he's alive!"

"Zoe we can't go out there! We can't!"

He was almost hysterical, but she took hold of his shoulders and shook him. "Shh! You want to wake the whole street?" she said and Mike took a steadying breath. "Todd would be out there right now looking for us –you said it yourself. Now we grab Brody and the map I've got and we go after Todd."

"You didn't see it Zo'! You didn't hear it in your mind. They want us to come for him. They know what we're up to. If you'd heard it you'd know that we don't stand a chance."

The night air whipped about them as the friends regarded each other. In the black of the night a low groan echoed from the bush. The pair slowly turned to the sound but it was what came next that sent them sprinting down the street.

A whisper not heard, but felt.

Join us… join us…

CHAPTER 26

From deep in the heart of the bush a strange call echoed. Pete stood in front of his archaic house, hands clasped over his ears, whispers dancing through the air. He had dreaded this moment even though he'd known it was coming. The creatures were casting their old spells.

He'd heard it some fourteen years ago. The creatures were cutting off the children from help. He just prayed they would heed his warnings.

Pete heard a creature slither around the edge of the clearing and steeled himself. It had come to torment him; to make him lose hope.

Please just take what you want and go back to your hole! He sent the thought out to the thing as it slithered to and fro in the shadows.

We will, it replied, *but first we will take the young ones – they will help us grow.*

He could almost see the thing smiling as it whispered in his mind. *I will stop you, I have before and I will again,'* he fired back. *Or have you forgotten that I know the words that can bring you to your knees?* Pete began to intone the ancient words that had kept the creatures from spilling out of the bush for the last fourteen years. But to his horror the creature did not retreat but stood firm.

Fool, it hissed, *this is our time; your words have no effect on us now. We will take the children of men; we will grow strong from them, and then we will punish man for taking our home!* It howled in his mind as it slithered into the clearing.

Pete dashed for the front door and threw himself inside. They could not hurt him in here; his power was too great in this sanctuary. And yet he heard the thing crawl onto the veranda and press its weight against the door.

And then we come for you, it whispered before it slithered into the bush.

Pete collapsed against the door, his head in his hands. He could not stop them.

CHAPTER 27

Something was very wrong; Brody could feel it. As the sun poked its head over the horizon the orange light streaked through the venetian blinds of his mother's bedroom.

Brody had been trying to rouse her since he had awakened from a dream he couldn't remember but had left him coated in sweat. His mother was breathing but she would not wake. He shook her but still she slept, peaceful and calm. He'd tried to call an ambulance but the phone was silent. He'd run to the neighbours' and banged on the door but no one had answered. He had not truly been afraid until he had tried almost every other house in the street with no answer.

He didn't understand what was happening; the sun continued to rise and no matter which street he ran down, he always seemed to end up back at his own street in front of his own house. Was he still trapped in a dream?

He had almost cried with relief when Zoe and Mike had appeared around the corner, and come running up to him, wearing the same mask of confusion and fear.

It was the same everywhere in the estate, they said. Mike had said that every road they had taken after leaving Zoe's house had been silent and still. Not a sound in the air or a sign of anyone. Mike had even thrown a rock onto someone's roof to see what would happen but no one had come to reprimand him, or even investigate the noise.

"We could see them," Mike said. "The people were all asleep."

"Even the air feels weird," added Zoe.

"What do we do?" Brody asked.

They wandered around the estate, but no matter which way they walked they ended up on the road that led to the empty lots. They even split up to try and find a way out but still they ended up back where they'd begun. They tried to retrace their steps but to no avail.

It was clear where they had to go; their choice had been made for them.

The air began to stir as they drew closer to the boundary fence; beyond it the bush seemed to be almost inviting. The stale silence of the estate seemed to be isolated behind them.

Zoe was first to step through the hole in the fence, Mike followed and when Brody stepped though that sinking feeling settled in his guts again. The three friends surveyed the bush before them.

"What the fuck is going on here?" whispered Mike.

"Watch the language," Zoe said calmly.

"Fuck that!"

"Keep it together and stay together," she said. "We head

for the centre – between the fence, the road and the river."

"How do you know?" asked Brody.

"Just trust me." She started walking down the hill toward the house. "Come on, we'll see if Pete is there."

"We'll make it back, won't we?" Mike asked.

"I won't let these things beat us," Zoe said over her shoulder.

"But… the creatures?" stammered Mike.

"We don't have a choice!" Her voice echoed off the hills. "Now come on."

Even the old ruins of the house seemed to be reserved; they looked through the windows and called out to Pete but there was no response.

"Why don't we make for the road and see if we can get help?" said Mike.

"If they can put that… spell, or whatever it is over everyone in the estate, then I'd say they can do much worse out here," Brody said putting a hand on Mike's shoulder. "It's just us, and them."

"Come on," Zoe said, "we gotta keep moving."

Brody looked back at the old house as they pushed on into the scrub. *Where are you Pete?* Had the old man done the smart thing and run? He didn't want that to be true, but Pete had told them not to interfere and now they were alone.

As the house disappeared behind, Brody heard movement ahead of them. They stopped, listened. No, they were *not* alone.

CHAPTER 28

From the turret window Pete watched as the children were swallowed up by the bush. A heavy feeling of helplessness overwhelmed him. He'd said he could help them but the creatures were stronger now than he'd thought. He knew the kids would come to him, but the boldness of the creature had terrified him. They were growing stronger, while he was growing weaker. He hid his face in his hands as the creatures' whispers drifted around his mind.

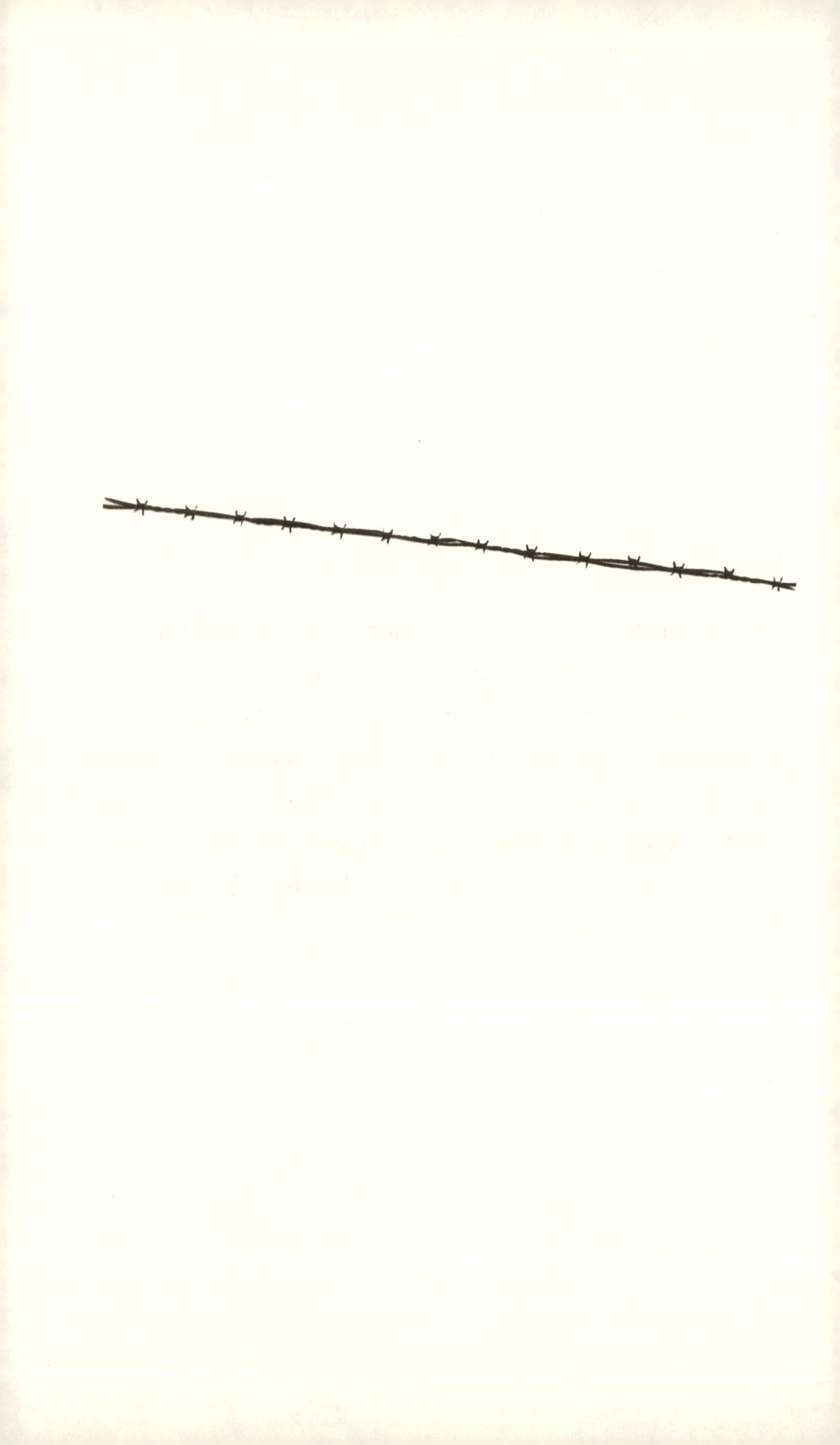

CHAPTER 29

The day grew hotter, and even Zoe's stoicism began to fade. When they passed a familiar, burnt-out gumtree – which they had passed twice before – they slumped in the oppressive heat. The once-welcomed summer sun had become their enemy.

"We need to rest," said Zoe.

The three of them sat in the shade of a huge blackberry bush. Brody picked some of the fruit and handed them around. They tasted like small slices of heaven in the dry heat; but they were hardly energising.

"We need to find some water," said Brody.

Mike pulled a small, half-empty bottle of Cola from his cargo shorts. "Here. It's flat and warm, but it'll have to do."

"I could kiss you," said Zoe before taking a healthy swig. She handed it to Brody who did the same. "We still need to find water though," she said. "Come on, I think if we head downhill we should hit the creek bed."

As they headed off Mike turned to look back at the Blackberry bush. "This is definitely the same tree," he stated, pointing at the thin, burnt-out trunk.

"Yeah," Brody agreed.

Mike looked at the tree and then to the bush, his face went pale. "We're sure?"

The realisation hit Brody as he and Mike locked eyes.

"Then where did these come from?" Mike said, gesturing to the bush. "They weren't there before."

"What are you saying? That the blackberries moved?" said Zoe.

A loud snap silenced her.

The three began to back away from the hollow tree as it uncoiled itself. Brody tried to yell for them to run but the words caught in his throat. The whispers rustled through the bush. The tree groaned. A deep, guttural sound shook the *real trees* around it. Birds took wing.

Suddenly, what Brody had thought was the bark of the tree, cracked open, revealing two pale, blank eyes. They burned into his. *I see you,* a voice whispered in his mind. The thing continued to twist itself free of the disguise.

Brody reached forward and grabbed Mike by the shirt. "Run!" he screamed.

The three of them dived head first through the bush, their arms and faces scratched and cut by branches and scrub as they scrambled away.

Behind them, the creature let out a deep, booming roar.

"The road! Head for the road!" yelled Mike.

"It's too far!" Zoe yelled back.

Brody dared glance over his shoulder; behind him trees

crashed aside as the twisted creature skittered after them. "Faster!" he screamed.

The terror in his voice seemed to spur his friends on. They dashed between the trees. The many branches ripping at their clothing, like the bush its self was trying to stop them. Blindly they pressed forward. Only the fear of being caught kept them moving. They ran and ran until their bodies gave out on them. Mike collapsed in a heap and Brody almost tripped over him.

"Mike! Get up! We have to keep moving!" Zoe yelled.

"I can't! Fuck, I can't move any further I… oh shit!" The three of them turned in unison, the trees swayed, one after the other, as the creature circled the group.

They couldn't see the thing, but the heavy crunch of leaves marked its progress. It stopped; and for the second time, Brody locked eyes with the creature through the swaying branches. Then it disappeared.

Zoe gripped his arm as Mike struggled to his feet. "Look," she said, and pointed to a fence line the other side of the valley, about a kilometre away. "That's the highway, if we can make it there we can…"

The creature roared again, the sound so loud the three of them had to cover their ears. When the sound had ceased bouncing off the many hillsides and valleys, the three friends removed their trembling hands from their ears. Then there came a distant reply.

CHAPTER 30

Brody's blood ran cold when another creature, closer, took up the call. Then another. Another. Until the roar seemed to be the only sound in existence. Trees shook, marking the path of the many creatures as they descended on the three.

"We've got to make it to the road," Mike yelled. "It's our only chance!"

Brody's gaze found the pale eyes of the creature again; it peered down at them from between the canopy.

A sickly, thin hand pushed aside a branch, revealing its dark face. When the whisper sounded in his mind he knew the thing was speaking only to him

Brave boy. Join us… Join your friend. Join him in the dark.

Brody turned and sprinted toward the road, as Mike grabbed Zoe and followed.

His legs burned and his lungs screamed, but Brody knew stopping would mean death. He chanced another glance behind him; strange, gangly shapes sprang through the trees in pursuit. They were horrible, twisted things that moved in ways no natural thing could.

Brody leapt over a fallen tree and skidded to a halt. What appeared to be an old mineshaft yawned open in front of him. He spun to warn the others when Zoe crashed into him as she tried to stop. For one terrifying moment Brody felt himself hanging in midair over the mineshaft.

He saw the panic in Mike's eyes and tried desperately to grab hold of his two friends, but only managed to ensnare Zoe. Mike began to get further and further away as he and Zoe fell into the dark.

CHAPTER 31

They tumbled for what seemed an eternity, bouncing off the rough, jagged sides before finally slamming to a stop. Brody drifted in and out of consciousness, his whole body throbbing with pain. Beside him, Zoe lay in a heap.

He thought he could hear Mike screaming his name from what seemed so very far away, but then the darkness closed in. When he came around, there was nothing but silence.

Zoe stirred next to him. "Brody…? You okay?" she stammered.

He reached out and gave her arm a squeeze to show he was awake. She tried to sit up, but slumped forward before the pair slid down a steep, muddy embankment into some sort of rock pool. The water was freezing and filthy, but the sudden cold and wet jolted them awake.

Zoe began to thrash in the water and Brody grabbed her around the waist and dragged her to the other side of the small pool. The pair lay panting on the muddy bank. Slowly Brody's eyes adjusted to the dark but it was the smell that really hit him – a putrid mix of dampness and rot.

"Are you hurt?" he whispered in a pained voice.

"Yes."

"Anything broken?"

"No. What about you?"

"I hit my head, but it's okay. My head's getting used to it," he said.

"What are those things?" she whispered.

"Let's not hang around to find out; we'll try and get back up to Mike."

They struggled to their feet, sore and dizzy from the fall, and inched their way around the filthy water to the opening. Brody stopped dead as a shadow passed across the light of the opening. Instinctively, he grabbed Zoe by the arm and pulled her beneath a dark outcrop beside the opening. He slapped his hand over Zoe's mouth as something slithered into the darkness.

For the first time, he saw the hideous thing clearly.

It seemed to have a serpent like body; its skin was ashen and brown. *Almost like burnt wood.* However, it was the front of its body that caused him to look away in repulsion. It looked human except for its thin frame, which slowly morphed into the serpent body further down. Its rangy arms bent in ways that no human limbs could. Brody shut his eyes and waited for it to pass. He heard it sniff the air, felt his heart beating against Zoe's back while she shivered in his arms. Eventually the beast slithered away and he opened his eyes only to see three more of the things hurry past. In their arms Mike hung like a rag doll.

Brody gently coaxed Zoe toward the opening. They tried

to climb toward the distant sunlight but the shaft was too steep. Calling for help would only alert the creatures to their presence, and besides, who could hear them? Now more than ever, Pete's warnings rang true – *'Stay out of the bush!'* With no idea of which way they should head, Brody and Zoe stumbled into the dark labyrinth of the caves.

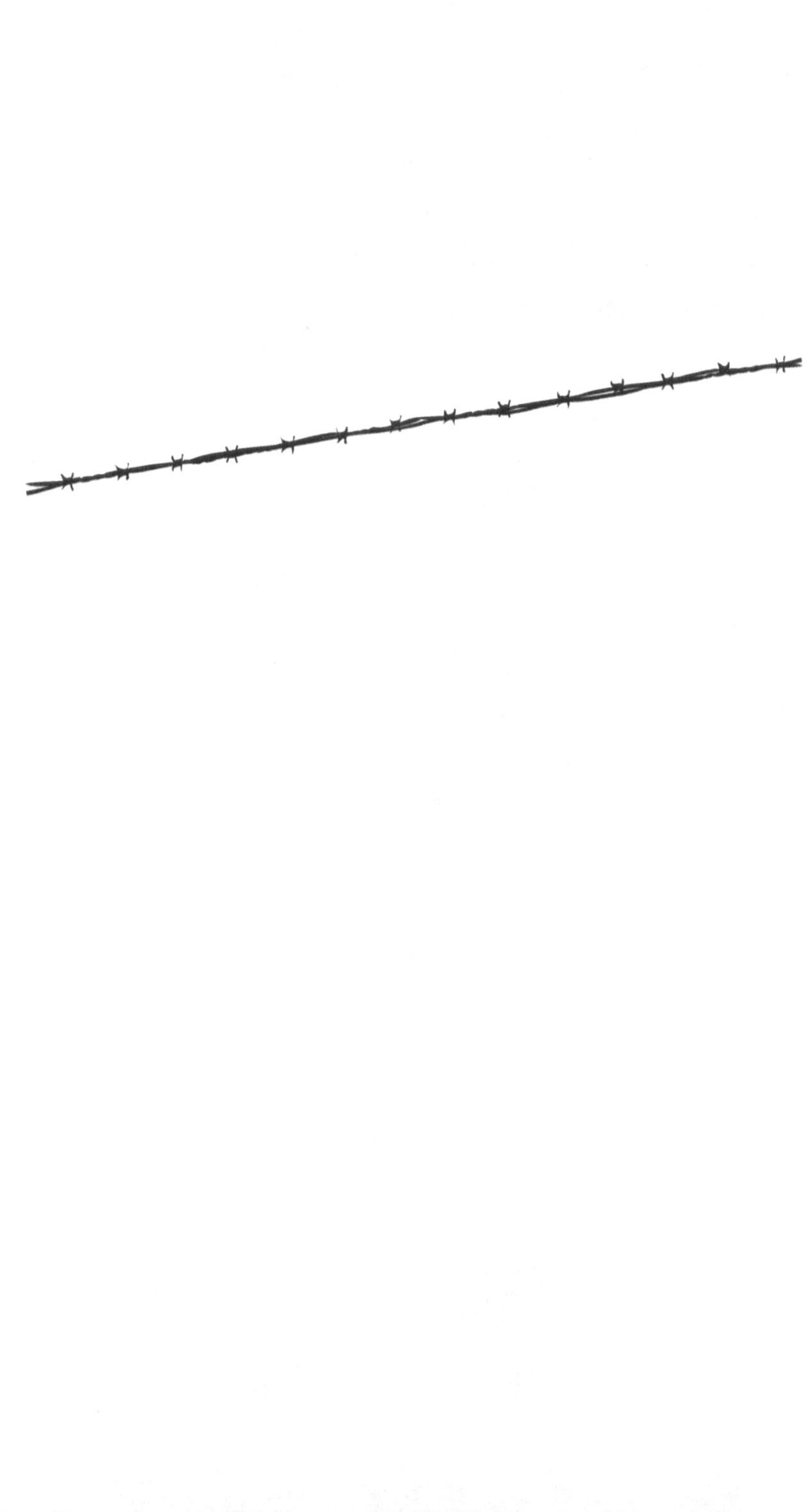

CHAPTER 32

rody and Zoe had been walking, and sometimes crawling, for hours. They were exhausted and the constant fear that they may round a corner, and bump into one of the serpent things in the dark was leaving them in a constant state of stress. But it was sadness that had spread its way through Brody. He had lost two friends; Todd and Mike were both dead. After seeing the creatures that took them, he was sure of it. What the hell had they been thinking? How could they fight things like that? Things they didn't understand; things that looked like no earthly creature any of them had ever seen before. Things that, according to Pete, had the power to make you simply walk into the bush and come straight to them.

They want you to come looking for them.

He remembered back to the newspaper clippings that Zoe had showed him. Years and years of disappearances, people never heard from again. Except there was one that had escaped…even though his sanity hadn't.

Be brave, don't give up, they haven't found you yet.

Zoe slipped from his grasp and slumped to the floor. Above

them, a single shard of light struggled through the cracks in the rocks. She looked up at it, her eyes squinting against the light.

"Come on, we have to keep moving," he said, trying to pull her back to her feet.

She whipped her arm from his grip. "I can't. I can't move any further," she said.

Her face was momentarily caught in the thin ray of light – she was badly dehydrated. Her eyelids were heavy and her shoulders slumped. His body was still stiff from the fall and he could do with a rest as well. Maybe they would be safe for a short while. He spotted a small tunnel off to the side where the earth looked soft and cool.

"Look, we'll be safe in there for a while," he whispered as he guided her toward the tunnel. She looked up at him, and he could almost read her thoughts – *we aren't safe anywhere*. The pair collapsed side by side in the dark. Zoe was out immediately, and he listened to her soft breathing to be sure she was okay then he, too, slipped into sleep.

CHAPTER 33

P ete stood on the back porch of the house and listened. The world was silent. Every now and then he would hear the song of a magpie somewhere in the distance, but apart from that, nothing. He threw his senses and thoughts into the surrounding bushland; he could feel its pulse, its life beating like a heart but when he turned his attention toward the estate beyond the boundary fence, there was nothing.

He stepped off the porch and hurried up the hill to the fence, and found the hole the kids used and stepped through, feeling every inch the ancient being he was.

It had taken him a long time to recover his courage, but now he steeled himself. He had to be strong; there was no other choice. He knew he couldn't stray far from the house for long. He could feel his strength slowly draining the further he went, but he had to know, he had to be sure... even though he had a fair idea of what was going on.

He walked the streets of the estate; the creature's spells crackled about the air, electric but unseen. He had never worked out how they managed to cast their...what should he call it? Magic? No, it was something more than that. He peered in some of the windows of the houses and saw the sleeping forms of the inhabitants. The spell was cast and none would wake until the creatures had finished with their business. As he walked back through the deserted streets to the boundary fence, his thoughts brooded on the children alone in the bush. They were simple targets, young and foolhardy.

When the estate had been built, Pete had despaired. The creatures would grow strong and one day they would be able to leave the bush. It was his curse to have to watch them growing stronger and bolder, while he grew weaker and weaker. Every fourteen years the cycle repeated. Humans went missing in the bush, and more of the odious creatures came into the world. Though they were weaker than when he had first dealt with them, they were definitely getting stronger. He had hoped the children would listen to him but he remembered the night he had saved Brody from the creature's scout. It still knew Pete had power, even though it was fading with every passing year. Anyone else would have gone mad from that encounter, but Brody had showed his mettle and got away.

Well, there was one other who had escaped them. But had he really? Pete left the estate and made his way back down the hill to the ancient house. He looked at the bush, and it looked back. No, he had not escaped them. Yes, he had escaped the caves long ago; he had made it back to civilisation but the people had called him mad when he spoke of what he saw – they had locked him away.

And when he escaped, he had come back to the old house and the bush. He had studied them and he had fought them.

He had trained his mind to fight against their strange powers; had learnt to cast spells of his own to protect the old house – his only sanctuary in the entire world. But the ancient powers he'd mastered, which kept him alive, were fading now. As he stepped off the veranda and headed into the bushland, he felt older than any man ever had. He would pass on soon, and the creatures would have won.

Pete might not have the power he once had, but he could try, with every last bit of his failing strength, he had to at least try. When Brody had been attacked, Pete had said he would not let them take this boy, not this time.

He would get those children back, even if it meant his death. After all, wasn't it better to die on your feet than to live on your knees?

Keep telling yourself that old man.

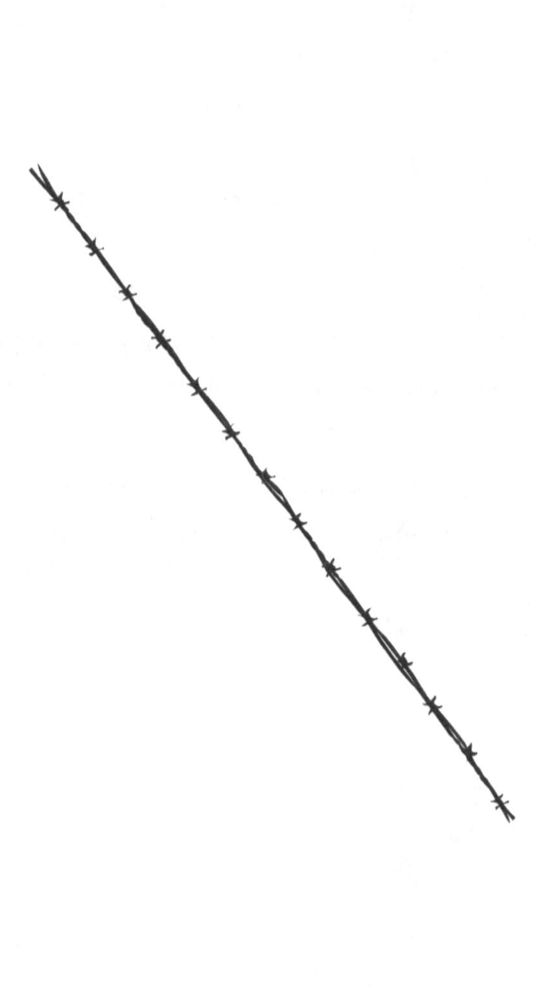

CHAPTER 34

A cool gust of wind brushed Brody's face, but while he woke his eyes remained shut. No, they were open! Why was everything so dark? He realised he was staring into the all-encompassing blackness of the caves. Zoe stirred beside him, her breathing deep and slow. He rolled away from her; the pain that had wracked his body had subsided but his head still throbbed. Warm, stale air surrounded him. It smelt bad, like rotting fruit and… Brody leapt to his feet, his blurred vision trying to focus on the thing not twenty centimetres from his face. His heart was beating so fast it felt like it would burst from his chest. The creature uncoiled itself and hissed; the stale, rotting breath hit him like a punch from his old man.

"Zoe! Run!" He dragged her by the scruff of her shirt out of the tunnel and into the pitch black of the caves. She turned, must have seen the slender, twisted shape of the creature rise up and screamed; the sound echoed through the cave system. They ran, bouncing off the walls like pinballs. Their skin was torn, their faces cut by the sharp stone walls. The creature followed almost leisurely.

Then the whispers started. The pair stopped in their tracks. For Brody, it didn't matter that every part of him wanted to run, he was pinned to the spot. It must have been the same for Zoe. The whispers were so loud in his mind that Brody thought he would go insane if they didn't stop.

Stay with us. Join us, brave little boy.

The creature slithered closer; it ran its rough, icy hands over both of them. Its fingers sent shivers down Brody's spine. So great was his fear that he began to cry. Beside him, Zoe stood like a zombie.

Here to stay with us now. Help us grow strong, come and see.

The creature's tail coiled around their legs then whipped their feet from under them. They landed hard on the cave floor and the creature dragged them deeper and deeper into the caves.

CHAPTER 35

Zoe had known fear in her life; the fear of not knowing if she would ever see her brother again, and the fear of having to accept the fact that he was gone. She knew the fear of leaving her family and being disposed to a boarding school in the city.

But this was true fear. The fear that comes with the realisation, that surely now, there was no hope of escape. She had been drifting in and out of consciousness for what seemed like hours. She felt broken, as the creature dragged them deeper and deeper into the caves. Her head swam in a sea of pain and the metallic taste of blood filled her mouth. Shock, she was in shock. Every now and then she heard Brody softly call to her but she just could not answer. They had never stood a chance against these things, and now they were going to die down here in the dark.

Suddenly the creature dumped them on the muddy ground. Zoe lay still until she was sure it had moved away.

"Are you all right?" she whispered to Brody.

"I'm sorry. I should never have let us go looking in the bush," Brody said, "We're as good as dead."

"Don't talk like that," she admonished. "If we give up now then–"

"We can't win this, Zoe," he cut in. "These things have played us right into their trap – we *are* as good as dead!"

Zoe surprised even herself with the slap. Her hand suddenly whipped out and smacked him across the cheek. "Don't you *dare*, Brody Webb! Don't you fucking dare give up on me now! I've lost two of my best friends to these fucking arseholes and I'm not going to lose you as well! Do you fucking understand me?"

She could sense his shock; hear him rubbing his cheek, but his breathing let her know he was alert now. *Nothing like a slap to set a man straight.*

"Zoe?" he said gently.

"What, Goddamn it?"

"That's the first time I've ever heard you swear."

They were silent, staring at each other through the gloom. Then both of them burst into laughter.

"Feels good, doesn't it," he said between laughs.

"Fuck yeah."

For a moment she almost forgot where she was until a low rumble shook the cave. Dust and small rocks fell from the cave's roof. A large tentacle shot out of the darkness and wrapped around Zoe's waist. It squeezed so hard that she vomited. It hoisted her into the air and threw her aside.

The last thing she heard before she hit the wall of the cave was the screams of her last surviving friend and the deafening roar of the creature as it descended on him.

CHAPTER 36

eak rays of light pushed their way through cracks in the cave's roof. Brody struggled as more and more of the large arms clutched at his body, lifting him high into the air. He screamed and thrashed in their grasp, but it was no good. He was too weak and his captors were too strong.

There must have been dozens of the creatures attacking him, but when he was drawn into the thin rays of sunlight it illuminated the awful truth.

He couldn't see all of the creature. Nor did he want to. However, he saw enough of its massive snake-like body and seemingly dozens upon dozens of arms, and its horribly misshapen head. It pinned him against the jagged rocks of the cave's roof then brought its face close. Two ice blue, pale eyes glared into his.

They call you the 'brave boy' I have been dreaming of you and your friends and now you are here to join us, it hissed in his mind. *Are you afraid, brave boy?*

Brody could not answer but it seemed the creature didn't need to hear his words. He could feel the thing in his head. It could hear his thoughts.

You are not as brave as my children made me believe, it seems. That is good, as we do not need your strength, only your body for us to feed on and grow.

The massive creature tossed Brody into a muddy pit as if he were an unwanted toy. The creature let out a low groan, and from one of the small outcrops another of the creatures appeared dragging something behind it – something pale and thin with a sickly bloated stomach. It was dumped in front of the behemoth, which then raised the poor thing up to Brody like a trophy.

In the dim rays of light, he saw what it was, but he wished he hadn't. This…*thing* turned its heavily sunken eyes on Brody and smiled.

Todd.

The once fit and healthy boy was now little more than a shell of his former self. Todd's mouth was opening and closing, trying to speak, but he was too weak and his voice was just a strained breath. And yet, somehow, he could understand what Todd was trying to say. He could read it in those bloodshot eyes.

I knew you guys would come.

The large creature let out a cruel chortle; it took one of its long fingers and drove it into Todd's grotesquely swollen belly. It ripped the soft flesh away. Todd found his voice. A throaty scream pummelled into Brody and he cried out helplessly as his friend's life faded in front of his eyes. But it was what fell from Todd's shredded stomach that silenced him.

Dozens and dozens of tiny, grey slugs tumbled to the cave

floor where they squirmed their way into a small pool of stale water. The large creature then flung Todd's lifeless body away like it was garbage. But Brody could not take his eyes off the slugs as they twisted in the pool. Two mature creatures stole from the darkness to watch them. One even plucked a few of the tiny slugs from the pool and held them like a mother would her newborn.

Their young! And a horrible realisation dawned on him. He was going to be next. The creatures were going to use him the same way they had used Todd. As if on cue the large creature spoke again.

You build your dwellings in our place. You build on top of our home! We will rise up and take it back, but first we must grow stronger!

Tears of terror, streamed down Brody's cheeks; he was the last one left alive and his fate would be that of Todd's. The massive creature then turned to gaze upon the pool of slugs. Brody cast his eyes across the cavern, to where Zoe laid broken and… She was moving! She was dragging herself across the jagged rocks, blood poured into her eyes from a deep cut in her forehead.

She was crawling blind, searching for a way out. As he watched the girl with the big green eyes, the girl who owned his heart, he found one more shred of strength to keep going.

He crawled across the filthy floor as the creatures continued to coo over their hideous newborns. Brody reached her and clutched her arm; she was about to scream but he quickly whispered reassurances in her ear.

"I can feel cool air coming from over there," she said and pointed to the mouth of a large tunnel.

"Then that's the way were going." He chanced a glance at the creatures but they were still occupied with their slugs. He pulled Zoe to a crouch and the pair supported each other's weight as they pressed on toward the tunnel.

"We can make it, Zo'"

"Todd?"

"He's dead, Zoe. They killed him," he heard her sob, once, then her arm tightened around his waist.

"Let's get the hell out of here," she said, a distinct note of determination in her tired voice.

He heard whispers, distant somewhere behind them. Then he saw it; a shadow crawling toward them. The pair froze, and Zoe made to turn back but he held her firm. "We can't go back that way," he whispered.

"What do we do? Try and sneak by it?"

"No more hiding. This time we fight," he replied.

He dropped to his knees and began to run his hand along the floor of the cave, until he found what he was looking for. His hand brushed against a smooth rock about the size of a cricket ball. He handed it to Zoe, who seemed to understand his intentions. He then searched the floor again, this time coming up with a jagged piece of stone about the same size. The shadowy thing crawled closer and closer, and Brody thought he could make out the twist of its tail. This one was a lot smaller than the others; maybe it was one of their young? A surge of energy pulsed through his body; here was an opportunity to exact some revenge for his friends.

The shadow drew closer and Brody roared and flung the stone with everything he had. He heard it smack into its target. Zoe hefted her missile above her head with both hands and threw it with deadly accuracy. It hit the creature's head with a resounding thud.

The shadow stopped crawling and lay still, for a moment all was totally silent. Then Brody heard a sound that sunk his heart.

It was a very human groan. He scurried forward on his hands and knees. He reached out and took hold of the shoulders, and the familiar voice spoke to him.

"I found you guys, I…finally found you…" Mike stammered. He was fading quickly. Brody could feel Mike's lifeblood draining away. He tried to cover the head wound, but it was so big. Zoe was there beside him, "Oh God, Mike, we didn't know! We didn't know! Please don't leave us…please!"

"We'll get you out," Brody said. "Just stay with us, okay? Don't go to sleep!" He tried to lift his friend, but Mike was too heavy and Brody was too weak.

Mike reached out and touched their faces. "You…you know how I got away from them?" he breathed.

"Shh…don't talk Mikey, we have to figure out how to get you out of here," Zoe said through her tears.

"No…no listen, it will save you…he…here!" Mike reached into his pocket and then pressed something small and metallic into Brody's hand. It was his Zippo. "Every time they came near me, I sparked…sparked it at them… and they ran like little bitches!" he turned to Zoe, "Excuse…my language Z-Zo'…"

She smiled, and held his hand tightly.

"If they come near you spark it at them…but hurry, there isn't much fuel left," he said.

Brody, made to lift Mike again, but his friend was still. He and Zoe were silent as Mike made a last gasp then his body went limp.

They sat over the body of their friend in silence. At the far end of the tunnel Brody heard the creatures approaching, their whispers becoming louder in his mind.

He turned to face them. There were three…no four…no six… Others moved about in the shadows and they whispered their strange words. The only thing he could hear clearly were the words, *Join us*, repeated over and over. They drew closer, stalking like great cats in the darkness. Brody held the lighter out in front of him and sparked it. The momentary illumination revealed the undulating mass. There were certainly more than six. The creatures hissed and shied away from the flashes of flame.

"You killed my friends, you bastards!" Brody cried. He strode forward continually sparking the lighter. Zoe followed close behind; she had picked up rocks and was throwing them as they went, screaming her rage.

They burst back into the large cavern; the creatures hissed and slunk around them, unsure whether to attack or not.

Zoe hurled the last of her rocks with full force at the biggest creature but it hit the monster and bounced harmlessly away. It tilted its great head and snorted.

Brody looked around them; they were completely surrounded. There seemed to be dozens of the creatures circling them. A strange calm came over Brody, and in the dark Zoe's hand wrapped around his. He was glad that it was her he was with.

The whispers came again, and his body went rigid as the creature's will overtook him.

Join us! Now is the time, join us!

He took a step toward the pit of slugs, and the creatures moved forward, one reaching for the lighter. This was it; they had won. He had failed. He gripped Zoe's hand tightly and waited for them to take him.

"Stop!" A gruff voice roared from the dark.

The whispers ceased and the creatures turned in unison to the speaker. Pete stepped from the tunnel entrance.

"You remember me?" the old man cried pointing at the great creature. It suddenly seemed agitated. No, it seemed afraid!

"Did I not say you would not take this boy? Not this time, and not while I still draw breath," Pete said.

The creatures converged on him, but he held his hands high and began to intone words that Brody did not understand, strange words. The creatures roared and hissed, twisting as if some unseen fire had burnt them.

"Brody!" Pete called. "Throw the flame into the pit! Hurry, I can't hold them for long.

One of the creatures launched its self at Brody but Pete roared his spell with even greater force and the creature clutched its' head, screaming.

Brody sparked the lighter, once, twice, but the flame wouldn't catch. Pete's spell was beginning to lose its hold. The largest of the creatures seemed to be concentrating all its will on him.

"Hurry boy!" he called. "I can't hold them off any longer!"

Brody tried again, but still the spark wouldn't catch. One of the creatures seemingly free from Pete's spell, tackled Brody hard. The lighter fell from his grip and he cried out in frustration. But in an instant Zoe snatched up the Zippo, and dashed toward the pool of slugs. Several of the monsters lunged for her but she launched herself at the pit, sparking the flame as she dived. She hit the oily water just as the flame sparked.

The pool ignited with a *whomp!* The creatures howled as their young went up in flames. Zoe was thrown back by the blast. The creature pushed Brody aside and scurried to the flaming pool. Pete seized the moment, and ran to Brody, dragging him from the flames. Only the largest made to chase after them, but Pete whispered something in a strange, chattering tongue and gestured with his hands. The pool exploded, the flames dowsing the creatures. Panicked; they ran this way and that as the flames spread.

Pete gripped Brody around the waist and hurried back to the entrance. The flames grew higher and higher. The creatures shrieked, as they tried to swat the flames, only to find themselves caught ablaze.

"Zoe! We can't leave her!" Brody called, Pete turned to see her struggling to her feet. She made to run… *WHOMP!* The flames exploded and sent her crashing out of sight.

"I'm so sorry, lad! We can't save her! We have to get out of here!" And with that Pete dragged Brody to the cave exit. The last he saw was the large creature tumbling into the flames; its flesh crackled and it howled as the flames grew and grew.

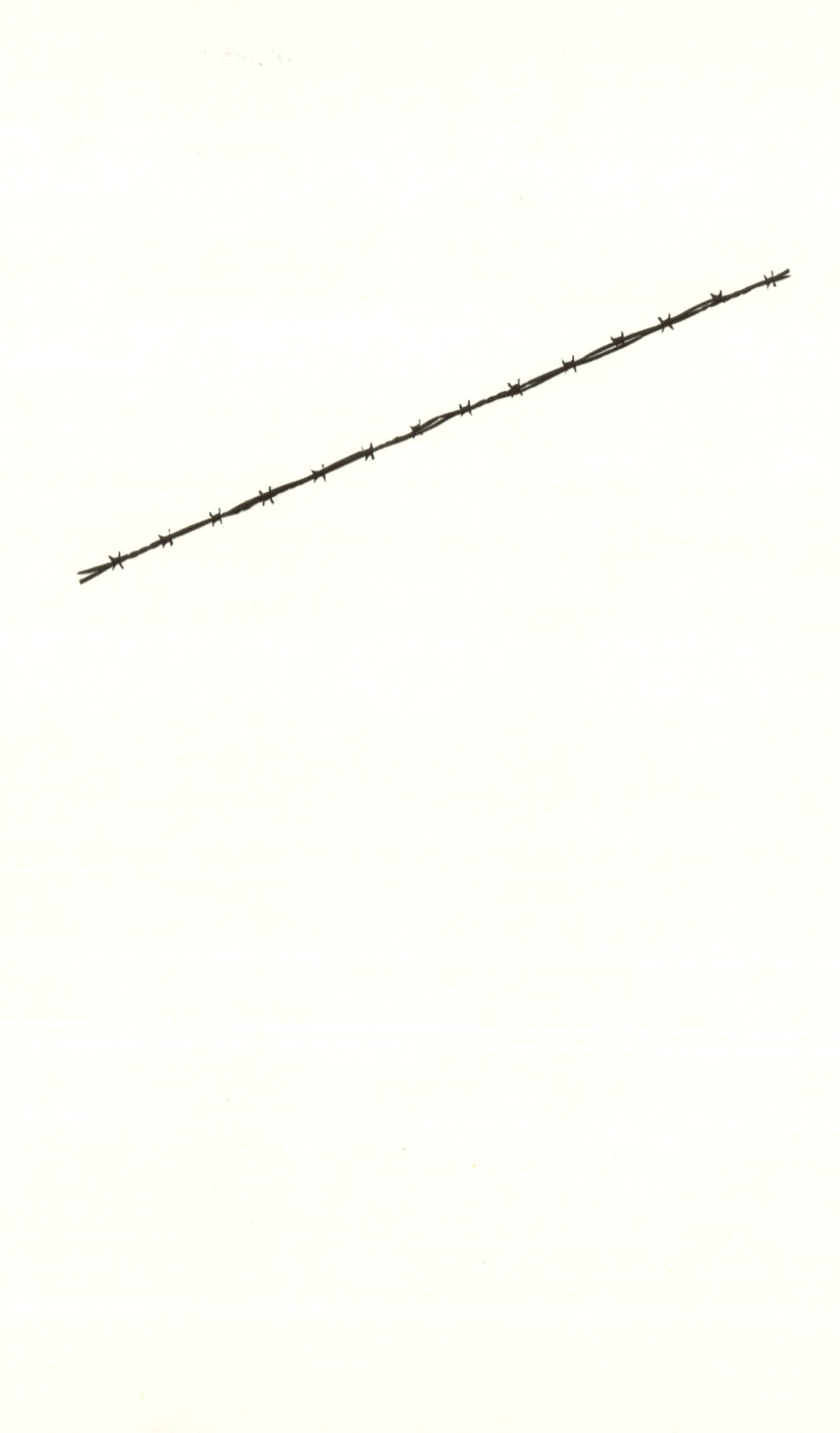

CHAPTER 27

Pete laid Brody down on the soft, long grass beneath the shade of a massive gumtree. Brody heard the old man slump beside him. The pair lay there, staring up at the clear blue sky. Every part of Brody's skinny body screamed in pain. He was covered in mud, deep cuts, and he was pretty sure he'd broken a rib or two. But none of that mattered to him because he was the last of the four friends. He had that last image of Zoe just before the blast blew her out of sight. Like a scratched record, it replayed over and over. That sinking feeling in his stomach would never leave him now. *Never.*

The smell of smoke was thick on the wind and he could hear the distant sound of sirens. The creature's spell over Golden Pastures must have been burned away when they were.

He turned to Pete. "Please tell me it's over."

Pete's clothing was torn and burned, his hair a complete mess. "Yes," he said, "it's over."

Distant voices drifted to him. The sirens were getting louder, too.

Pete put a hand on Brody's shoulder. "I have to leave you

now, lad. Sounds like the cavalry is coming."

"Did Zoe…is she…?"

He looked away. "I'm sorry. I didn't want it to end like this." He stood and looked at the sky, breathing deeply. "Brody, whatever you do, don't let them…" he gestured in the direction of the sirens, "…discover what the truth is. They're not ready for it. I tried to make them understand when I escaped but they thought I was mad."

"Then what do I tell them?"

"Tell them you went searching for your friend and got lost. You started the fire to get their attention…anything! Just don't tell them about…our *friends*."

"But if you stay, and you tell the truth…"

"My time is done, lad. I've used it all up," he said. "Keep an eye on the bush, watch for them." He suddenly doubled over; the sirens we're getting closer now. Brody heard the sound of trucks somewhere down near the fire.

"Pete?"

"I have to go, son," he said and stumbled off into the thick bush.

"Pete! Wait!" The old man turned. "Thank you," Brody said.

Pete smiled and struggled off. Brody lay back and waited as the voices neared. He would have cried for his friends but, mercifully, he drifted into unconsciousness.

CHAPTER 28

He awoke on the crisp sheets of a hospital bed. The smell of disinfectant was thick in the air, the room was quiet, and sunlight poured through the cracks in the blinds. Brody was covered in bandages; he felt tired, but calm.

A warm hand wrapped around his arm, and he turned to see his mother smiling at him. "Hey brave boy, how are you feeling?" she said softly.

"Mum…I couldn't save them, I tried but…"

"Shh, it's all right." She leant in close. "They found Zoe. She crawled out of some cave and…"

He sat bolt upright. "I have to see her! Is she okay?"

His mother put a restraining hand on his chest. "She's resting, love, you'll see her soon enough." Tears welled in her eyes. "I woke and thought I'd lost you, that you'd run away or something. Then when we all saw the smoke coming from the bush, I thought…I thought…"

He put his arm around her. "I'm sorry. We just wanted to find Todd but we just made it worse."

"But sweetheart, Todd is…what do you mean made it worse?"

"We…we lost Mike," he said. The memories of his friend's death flashed in his mind.

He was about to tell it all to her – the creatures, their cave beneath the bush, and what they had done to Todd when there was a knock at the door.

Two suited men entered, one carrying a bulky folder under his arm. They smiled and he saw the flash of police badges on their belts. The one with the folder closed and leant against the door. The other, who looked slightly older, pulled up a chair and sat by Brody's bed.

"Hi Brody, I'm Detective Saunders. My partner and I have been investigating the fire that happened in the bush the other day."

Brody didn't hesitate, "It was us…me! I started it."

The detective turned to his partner. "Well, that was probably the quickest confession we've ever got!"

"Is my son in trouble, officer?" his mum said, placing a protective arm around him.

"Well, we will need to take a statement at some point. But your friend Zoe says you were trying to signal for help and it got out of control," he said raising a questioning eyebrow.

"That's right," Brody nodded. "But I started it!"

"Zoe says she did," Saunders replied. Brody went to speak again but the detective waved him quiet. "It's all right, she told us the whole story. It was brave of you to go looking for your friend, but now your other friend is missing, isn't he?"

Brody hung his head, the detective scratched his chin as if in thought. "Look Brody, we're not here to give you a lecture, you'll have to answer for the fire, but we understand there were reasons behind it." He patted Brody's leg. "We'll let you get some rest. However, there is just one thing." Brody looked up at the policeman. "When we first spoke to your friend, she mumbled something about being trapped in a cave. She was a bit out of it, but she mentioned that an old man was there. Does the name, Pete, mean anything?"

Brody said nothing.

"Also, some of your wounds are consistent with injuries from common assaults, being slapped or punched." He leant forward. "Brody, did this old man hurt you or your friends? You can tell us, mate. We want to help you, understand?"

"He was trying to help *us*! He wasn't hurting us, Pete warned us not to go into the bush, but we didn't listen. We should've listened!" Tears streamed down his face; tears that had been building like water trapped behind a dam.

"I think that's enough questions for now," his mother said, standing to bundle the policemen out the door.

"Just one last thing," said the younger detective as he pulled a large photo from his file. He held it up to Brody. "Is this the old man?"

The picture was a kind of mug shot, and the man in the picture was Pete – there was no doubting it. But, he looked much younger.

Brody looked from the picture to the policeman. "No," he said. But he could tell the policeman knew he was lying.

The policeman sighed and stepped out the door. "Thank you for your time, Brody. Mrs Webb, could we speak outside for a moment?"

She nodded and followed them, closing the door behind her.

Brody wiped the tears from his eyes and listened as best he could to their conversation. But he could only make out snippets.

"Who the hell is that?"

"…that old house belonged to him…"

"…near where we found the body of that hiker…we thought it was the boy, Todd…"

"Is this old bastard the one who did this to my son?" his mother asked.

"…matches the description given by the other kid…"

"…can't be though…"

"Why?"

"…been dead for years…"

CHAPTER 39

Storm clouds were gathering as Brody loaded the last of his belongings into the back of his mum's hatchback. They'd sold off most of their stuff; only keeping the bare essentials. He didn't know how he really felt about moving again. He knew it was good for his mum, and really, he'd only loved Golden Pastures because his best friends lived here, and they were gone now.

Except for Zoe of course, but he'd only seen her a couple of times in the weeks since they'd left hospital.

"All done?" his mother called from the house.

"All done," he said quietly.

She locked the front door and made her way over to him, draping an arm around his shoulder. "One last look?" she said, "The place your uncle has set up for us is at least twice this size."

He nodded.

"Brody, I know this has been hard. I can't imagine what the loss of…" she trailed off. "Look," she continued after a moment, "it's not going to be easy, sweetheart, but together we can do this.

And maybe, when your dad's...better, he'll come down too."
He smiled at her, and she ruffled his hair. "Come on, let's hit the road."

"Brody!"

He turned to see a figure gliding down the road on her bike. She pulled to a stop and dumped it on the lawn. Under her arm she carried a frame. The green-eyed girl smiled at him.

Zoe was looking fresh, even though she was still sporting some nasty bruises and burns. She'd had to cut her hair right back as most of it had been burned off in the fire.

"I'll give you a moment," his mum said with a wink, before smiling at the girl. "Hi Zoe!"

"Hi Mrs Webb," she said in that practiced private schoolgirl voice.

Brody's mum jumped in the car and backed it out of the drive.

"Hey," he said, as she got closer.

"Hey."

"How are you feeling?"

"Better; still get headaches, though. But I think this stupid hair cut is worse than any of the cuts and burns."

"I think it looks good on you," he said. "Though your ears stick out a bit."

She laughed. "Is that so?"

There was a rumbling in the distance and both of them jumped slightly, but it was only the coming storm.

"I'm sorry we left you, Zoe. We thought you were... well..."

"It's okay, at least we stopped them," she said. "You have

to promise me one thing, and I'll promise the same."

"Anything."

She took his hand. "Don't become a stranger, stay in touch. I don't want to lose you, Brody."

"You won't, I promise."

She hugged him. "I miss them so much," she said.

"Me too."

She handed him the frame. It held a picture of the four friends, looking bright and care-free. "I've got the same one over my bed at home."

"Thank you," he said, holding back the tears that threatened to spill. "I'll hang it there, too."

She kissed him on the cheek, and gave his arm a squeeze, like she didn't want to let go. "Brody, Pete…is he…"

"He's gone…well as far as I know."

She nodded. "Then it's up to us to keep a look out for…" she glanced to the distant bush line, "…you know what."

The storm rumbled again. "You better get home," he said softly.

She hugged him once more, and he hugged her back just as fiercely. "Get out of here," she said, "before you make me cry."

"I'll call you, I promise."

"You better!"

She waved at Brody's mum, who waved back then he watched her hop on her bike and peddle away. Without a look back, he jumped in the car and his mother pulled away from the curb and headed for the highway.

"You all right, love?" she asked.

He smiled. "I'm fine, Mum." He rested his head against the window, clutched the picture to his chest and closed his eyes.

Behind them, the storm broke.

CHAPTER 40

In the deep heart of the bush, a small bird sat on a tree, happily pruning its feathers just as the rain began to fall. It fluttered its wings, and was about to head for the cover of its nest when a long slender hand whipped out from the tree and took hold of it. The bird was crushed, in an instant.

The tree cracked and twisted as it uncoiled its self. It hissed and dropped the bird into its mouth, swallowing it whole. The other birds close by, flew into the air, desperate to get away from the thing that was clearly not a tree.

The creature watched them go. It was hungry and cold, but it could not return to the burnt out caves it had once called home. Not yet anyway. It would take a long time to clear out the damage the small humans and the old human had made, and it wasn't strong enough for that yet. It was only now starting to recover from its burns. It had been lucky to escape and it knew it. Only one other of its kin had managed to flee the flames – it was foraging down the valley somewhere.

They would need to be patient if they meant to rebuild their colony. They would have to wait and…

The creature's thoughts were interrupted by the sound of boots crunching over the wet ground below it.

Two humans stepped out from the bushes. They wore bright suits, like the humans who put out the fire that had spread from the cave.

"We'll have to check out those caves another time," said one.

"Yeah, the weather's turned nasty," said the other. "Let's just rest for a couple of minutes and then we'll head back to the estate."

"Good thing the fire didn't spread too far. Would've been a disaster in the making."

And they sat down, right at the creature's feet, and continued to chatter.

If the creature could have laughed out loud, it would have, this was too easy. It concentrated its mind on the humans and sent out its simple message.

Join us, join us, join us…

ABOUT THE AUTHOR

Stefan was born in Adelaide, South Australia. He moved to Melbourne, where he graduated from the Victorian College of the Arts, as an actor. Since graduating he has appeared in Television, Radio, Film and Theater productions. He has also written two feature film scripts, both currently in pre-production.

www.facebook.com/Stefan-Taylor-Authorscreenwriter

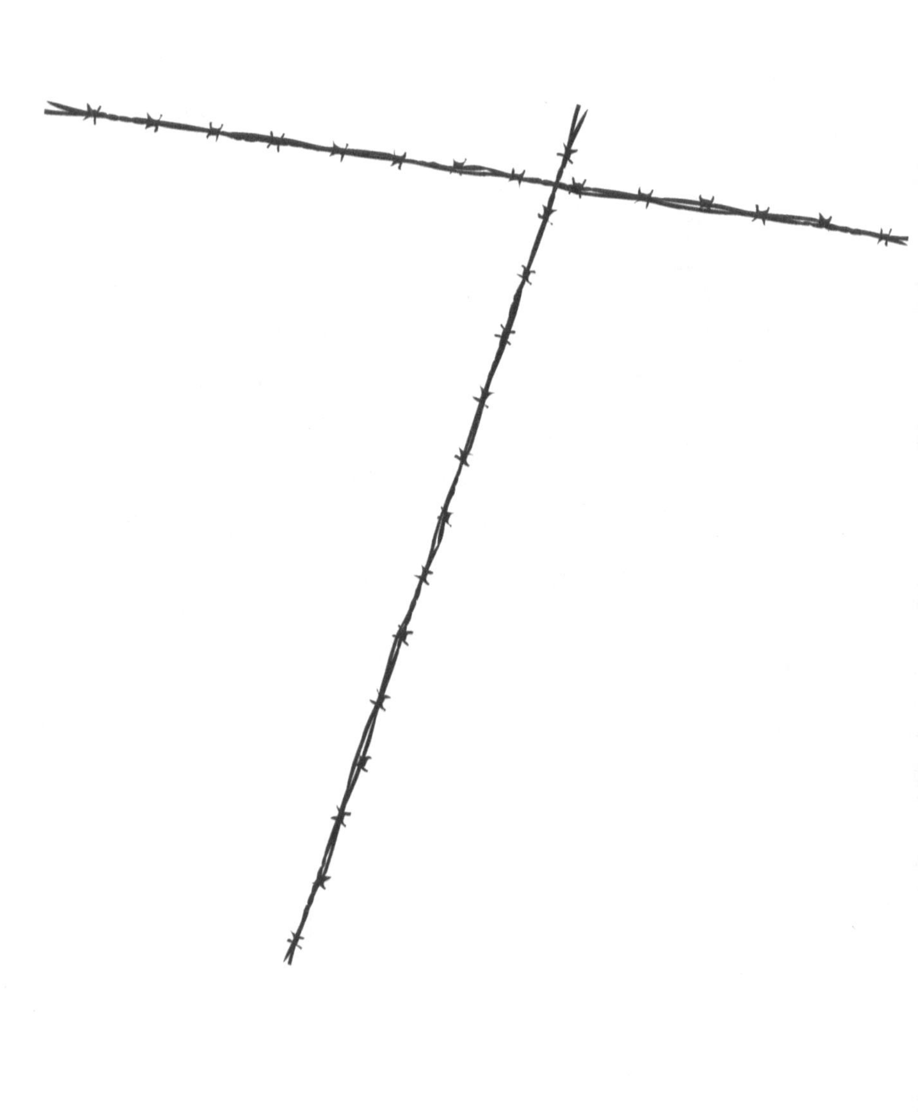

ACKNOWLEDGEMENTS

My thanks must first go to Amanda J. Spedding, for her amazing positivity and support. To David Schembri for his outstanding cover design. And finally to Meredyth Taylor who, after reading the first draft said, "You should add more monsters."

So I did.

Sick Little Pupplies by Stefan Taylor and Simon J Green

A collection of short horror stories you can rip through in hours, but will haunt you for days.

Demons that draw on a family's misery. The violent deaths of clients from hell. Serial killers and cursed cures that don't turn out how you'd expect. Stefan Taylor builds dark worlds full of classic tension and fear. Simon J Green weaves visually rich tales of carnage and humour. Together, they bring you previously published work alongside original stories designed to scare, shock, and make you feel sick.

https://www.amazon.com/Sick-Little-Puppies-horror-collection-ebook/dp/ B07DHXCHY8

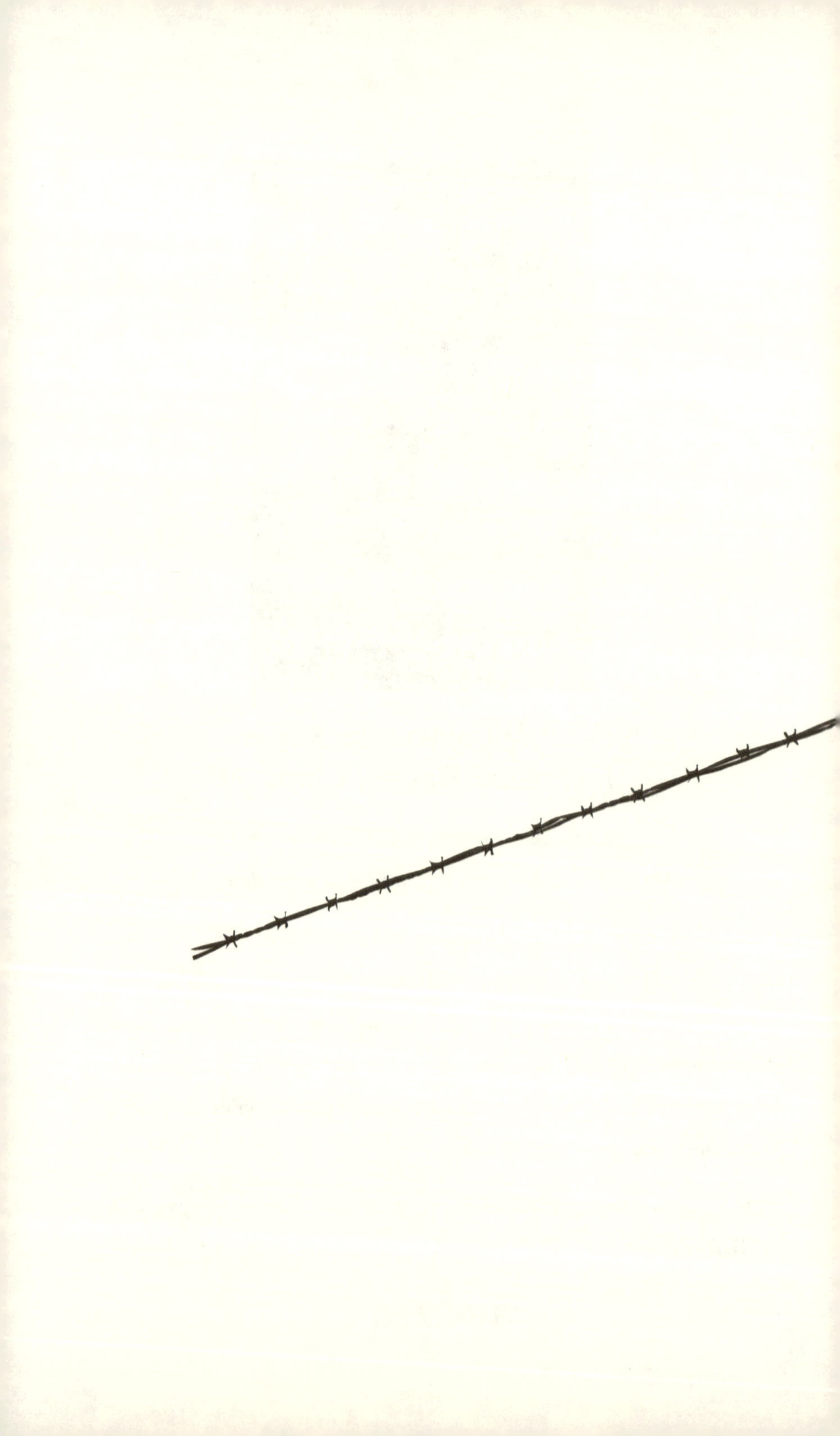

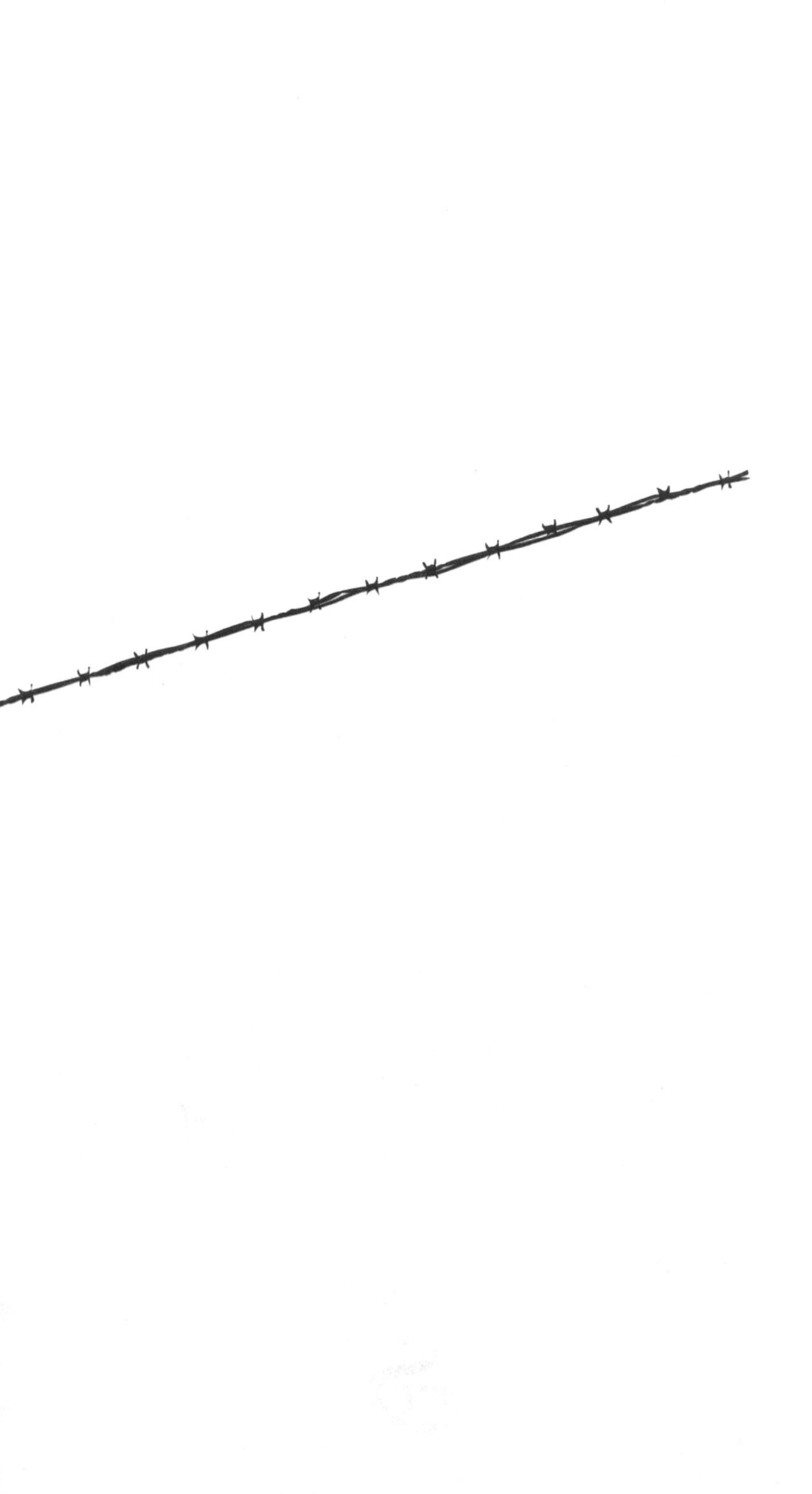